ALI
CROSS
THE SECRET DETECTIVE

JIMMY PATTERSON BOOKS FOR YOUNG READERS BY JAMES PATTERSON

Ali Cross

Ali Cross

Ali Cross: Like Father, Like Son

Ali Cross: The Secret Detective

Daniel X

The Dangerous Days of Daniel X

Daniel X: Watch the Skies

Daniel X: Demons and Druids

Daniel X: Game Over

Daniel X: Armageddon

Daniel X: Lights Out

Dog Diaries

Dog Diaries

Dog Diaries: Happy Howlidays

Dog Diaries: Mission Impawsible

Dog Diaries: Curse of the Mystery Mutt

Dog Diaries: Ruffing It

Dog Diaries: Dinosaur Disaster

House of Robots

House of Robots

House of Robots: Robots Go Wild!

House of Robots: Robot Revolution

I Funny

I Funny

I Even Funnier

I Totally Funniest

I Funny TV

I Funny: School of Laughs

The Nerdiest, Wimpiest, Dorkiest I Funny Ever

Jacky Ha-Ha

Jacky Ha-Ha

Jacky Ha-Ha: My Life Is a Joke

Jacky Ha-Ha: A Graphic Novel

Jacky Ha-Ha: My Life Is a Joke (A Graphic Novel)

Katt vs. Dogg

Katt vs. Dogg

Katt Loves Dogg

Max Einstein

Max Einstein: The Genius Experiment

Max Einstein: Rebels with a Cause

Max Einstein Saves the Future

World Champions! A Max Einstein Adventure

Middle School

Middle School: The Worst Years of My Life

Middle School: Get Me Out of Here!

Middle School: Big Fat Liar

Middle School: How I Survived Bullies, Broccoli, and Snake Hill

Middle School: Ultimate Showdown

Middle School: Save Rafe!

Middle School: Just My Rotten Luck

Middle School: Dog's Best Friend

Middle School: Escape to Australia

Middle School: From Hero to Zero

Middle School: Born to Rock

Middle School: Master of Disaster

Middle School: Field Trip Fiasco

Middle School: It's a Zoo in Here!

Treasure Hunters

Treasure Hunters

Treasure Hunters: Danger Down the Nile

Treasure Hunters: Secret of the Forbidden City

Treasure Hunters: Peril at the Top of the World

Treasure Hunters: Quest for the City of Gold

Treasure Hunters: All-American Adventure

Treasure Hunters: The Plunder Down Under

Becoming Muhammad Ali (cowritten with Kwame Alexander)

Best Nerds Forever

Laugh Out Loud

Not So Normal Norbert

Pottymouth and Stoopid

Public School Superhero

Scaredy Cat

Unbelievably Boring Bart

Word of Mouse

For exclusives, trailers, and other information,
visit Kids.JamesPatterson.com.

JAMES PATTERSON

JIMMY PATTERSON BOOKS
LITTLE, BROWN AND COMPANY
New York Boston

The characters and events in this book are fictitious. Any similarity to real persons, living or dead, is coincidental and not intended by the author.

JIMMY Patterson Books / Little, Brown and Company
Hachette Book Group
1290 Avenue of the Americas, New York, NY 10104
JamesPatterson.com

First Edition: June 2022

JIMMY Patterson Books is an imprint of Little, Brown and Company, a division of Hachette Book Group, Inc. The Little, Brown name and logo are trademarks of Hachette Book Group, Inc. The JIMMY Patterson Books® name and logo are trademarks of JBP Business, LLC.

Library of Congress Cataloging-in-Publication Data
Names: Patterson, James, 1947– author.
Title: The secret detective / James Patterson.
Description: First edition. | New York ; Boston : Jimmy Patterson Books/Little, Brown and Company, 2022. | Series: Ali Cross | Audience: Ages 10–14. | Summary: "Ali Cross and his friends chase police cases while Ali is caught up in a debate about policing." —Provided by publisher.
Identifiers: LCCN 2022004087 | ISBN 9780316409919 (hardcover) | ISBN 9780316410014 (ebook)
Subjects: CYAC: Police—Fiction. | Debates and debating—Fiction. | Middle schools—Fiction. | Schools—Fiction. | African Americans—Fiction. | Washington (D.C.)—Fiction. | LCGFT: Novels.
Classification: LCC PZ7.P27653 Sd 2022 | DDC [Fic]—dc23
LC record available at https://lccn.loc.gov/2022004087

ISBNs: 978-0-316-40991-9 (hardcover), 978-0-316-41001-4 (ebook)

Printed in the United States of America

LSC-H

Printing 1, 2022

ALI
CROSS
THE SECRET DETECTIVE

CHAPTER 1

I'M GOING TO start by telling you about my friend Gabe Qualls. He's a part-time middle school student and a full-time genius. Because he's a genius, he's always inventing things. And because we're such good friends, he's always sharing the inventions with me.

Just last week he perfected one of his best inventions ever. It arrived at the best possible time. You see, I haven't had a decent real adventure in what feels like a hundred years. I've been hurting for something exciting to happen. And Gabe's new invention is practically a guarantee that something big will happen.

Here's what it is. A cell phone that lets me intercept police calls.

Wait. Wait. Wait. It's nothing bad. Nothing illegal. I mean, come on. My father is Detective Alex Cross. With him as a dad, I've got to be extra careful.

Here's the deal. Gabe figured out how to make an app that actually transcribes and summarizes local police radio chatter in real time. (Don't ask me how he did it. *He's* the total computer genius. Not me.)

But here's the coolest part. Gabe secretly hooked it up to the Washington, DC, Metropolitan Police scanner. And he set it so if the cops say certain key words, or if they're headed somewhere in our neighborhood, it sends a ridiculously loud text alert to both our phones. So whenever there's an emergency call in Southeast—the part of the city where me and my family live—we're the first two to hear about it.

Which means we can get to the crime scene fast.

Oh, it works well—really well. In fact, I'm in a

deep cozy sleep this morning and . . . there it is now. Loud. Blaring.

I look at my phone. 3:35 a.m. The screen simply says:

Stanton Houses. Emergency situ. Group.

Group? What does that mean? Gabe really needs to work on an in-app translator for the police lingo.

Moaning just a little, I stumble out of bed and slip into my jeans and a ratty gray T-shirt. I've chased after three police calls so far this past week. A stolen car, an attempted robbery, and a boring noise complaint. Each one had potential, but they all turned out to be duds.

I'm hoping this new call is an exciting one.

Chasing police calls is kind of a weird hobby, right? Most of my friends play video games. Or sports. Or make goofball TikTok videos.

Me? I like to check out crime scenes. Let me rephrase that. Checking out crime scenes, looking into police cases, well, that's about the coolest thing I can imagine.

Why do I do it? I guess you could say it's in my DNA. Yeah. That's it. But even if that's the reason,

I don't think the guy responsible for that DNA, my dad, would be cool with me following in his footsteps, especially since I'm still in middle school. Crime, guns, bad guys. It can be a dangerous job.

Which is why I'm forced to sneak out of the house. *Shhhh.*

Holding my dirty Puma Clydes in my hand, I soft-step down the stairs and tiptoe out the door. If I wake him or my stepmom, Bree, I'm dead. My family, you see, is pretty good at hearing stuff, seeing stuff, and, like me, gently nosing into one another's stuff.

Luckily, this time, they all seem to be sleeping like a bunch of babies.

I wait till I'm a whole block from my own house before I call Gabe.

"Are you ready to go?" I ask.

I can tell from his grumpy voice that Gabe hasn't moved since *his* own police scanner alert went off.

"It's like three o'clock in the morning, Ali," he says.

I fight his grumpy with the best friend card.

"C'mon, man. You wouldn't let me go alone,

would you?" There's an address on the screen now. I read the message to him. "Group disturbance at 1916 18th SE."

Then I tease him a little. I can't help it.

"Come on, Gabe. It's your favorite part of town."

"Public housing? The Stanton Houses? My favorite part?"

"Yeah," I answer. "It's right across the street from the *library*."

"Funny stuff, Ali. Nothing like a nerd-genius joke at three in the morning."

"Just get your butt over there," I say. "Now."

"It's probably just like the others. A big nothing deal," Gabe says.

I know Gabe could be right. Maybe this call *will* turn out to be another dud.

But for some reason, I have a feeling it's going to be a big one.

Chapter 2

GABE AND I meet up. The genius looks like he's still dressed for bed—red boxers sticking out from green gym shorts, along with a red-and-white striped T-shirt.

"What's up, Christmas tree?" I say.

"Huh?" He doesn't get the joke. Or at least he pretends not to.

We hustle over toward the crime scene. It's not hard to find. It's all flashing lights and megaphones. It's a nasty mix of police shouts and wailing sirens.

Then we plant ourselves by the side of the library for the perfect view.

"This looks pretty serious," I say.

"Uh, you think so?" Gabe says. "What gave it away? The eight police cars or the forty people crowding around?"

I guess I am a master of the obvious.

"It's got to be something with the gangs," Gabe says.

As soon as Gabe mentions the word *gangs*, I tell him what my dad once said.

"If you can bust the gangs, you can build the city."

"Man, it would take a lot of busting and a lot of building," Gabe says, and as I look across the street at the twisted window bars and graffiti on the Stanton Houses, I know what he means.

The biggest problems with the gangs are the feuds between the gangs themselves. The fights can be brutal—guns, fists, knives, even rocks are used. They're started over turf disputes or drugs or someone's girlfriend or boyfriend.

Police are leading a few folks out of the building.

It's pretty clear that these are residents of the houses. Adults wearing nightgowns and underwear and sweatpants. Little kids in pajamas.

The police rush this small group to a spot behind one of the barricades. Then we hear a guy on a megaphone talking to the people watching from the surrounding houses: "PLEASE REMAIN IN YOUR HOMES. PLEASE REMAIN IN YOUR HOMES. POLICE WILL INFORM YOU WHEN IT'S SAFE TO LEAVE."

"That'll sure scare you," Gabe says.

I check my phone. "No updates on the event," I tell Gabe. "I think we should remain in our current position."

Gabe rolls his eyes. His voice is really sarcastic as he says, "Yes, sir. Whatever you say, Sergeant Ali." Before I can tell Gabe off, we see a sudden parade of people coming out the side door of the apartment.

Three of those people—two guys, one woman—are clicked into handcuffs. It looks like stuff you see in news clips. The police stare straight ahead while they walk. The suspects are pushing their chins into their chests as far as they can. I watch closely as the handcuffed people are escorted by an even mix of four uniformed cops and four plainclothes.

Okay. I'm excited, excited enough that I decide to move in closer to the front of the crowd.

"Cool it, man," Gabe says as he tugs at the back of my shirt. "The police don't want any interference from two punk teenagers."

Gabe is right. Plus, some of the officers and detectives might actually recognize me. I've been down at headquarters a few times with my dad. We move back a little, a pretty bad attempt at camouflage.

Three police cars pull up to the side of the building where the action is.

"Three perps. Three arrests. Three squad cars," I say. "Everybody gets their own chauffeur. This must be serious."

"Hey, Ali. Look at the second guy," Gabe says. He sounds anxious.

"Lower your voice, man," I say.

"On the right. On the right," he says. He doesn't really talk any quieter. Instead he talks in the kind of whisper you could hear a few yards away. "Look at the second guy on the right."

I squint. I look.

Oh, damn! Damn and damn it again.

"Let's move," I say. We bend over, put our heads down, and we look exactly like what we are—two scared, stupid kids trying to hide.

"You said they were all asleep when you left your house," Gabe says.

"They were. At least I thought they were," I answer.

"Man, you better hope he doesn't look this way. Nobody can fool your father."

"Least of all me," I say.

CHAPTER 3

THE POLICE LOAD the three people into three separate patrol cars that flip on their sirens and drive off. It's kind of interesting to watch how the officers handle the three people that they're bringing in. They're not really rough with them. There's no shoving or pushing. But they're firm also. I'd call them confident but polite. I do notice that one of the officers does not do the usual "watch-your-head" move when they put their guy into the car.

I wonder, is that a television thing? Or is it an actual rule, that the officer just broke?

I'm pretty sure that Gabe and I are far enough away that nobody can see us. And my father wasn't really looking around; he seemed very preoccupied with walking with, watching, and guiding his suspect.

I don't even realize I've been holding my breath until he gets into an unmarked car and drives off, too.

"We can move in closer now," I say.

"Yeah," says Gabe. "Now that the big guy is gone."

I'm not sure, but I'm not liking Gabe calling my father "the big guy." It's not exactly disrespectful. And, okay, the name sort of fits. But my friend's voice has a little scorn to it. Maybe. Yeah, maybe. It could be I'm just too sensitive.

Anyway, as we cross the street, I scope out the crowd. I'm guessing most of these people are from the Stanton Houses. Probably some are what the police call "lookie-loos," the people who gather around when there's a car accident, a fire, or even an extra-dangerous crime scene, like a shooting. Why watch Netflix when you can watch real life?

A really old guy standing next to Gabe, smoking a pipe, says, "You kids from the neighborhood?"

"Yeah, pretty close by," I say.

"But not *that* close," Gabe says. I don't know what he's worried about that he has to add that little bit. Not that the old guy seems to care.

"Bad stuff is always going on around here," says the old guy. "Nobody can stop it."

"It's the gangs again," says a woman who's holding a very unhappy baby. The baby is screaming loud enough that she could actually drown out the sirens on the police cars that are speeding away.

The woman talks over her baby. "He's right. It's the same as always. The gangs fight. Some of 'em get arrested. But nothing changes. Same old story." Then she adds, "I wish all the gangs would just kill each other already. Then we'd be done with it."

The old guy nods his head. "Sometimes it seems that that's exactly what they're trying to do. Kill each other. Can't say as I'd be heartbroken if they all ended up dead."

I want to cry out, *What are you, crazy? What kind of solution is that?*

"Cops'd just as soon let them run around as shoot them," says the young mother.

"Cops don't care," says the old man.

Okay, my blood is at boiling level now. I want to say, *The police try really hard to keep things under control. And—you know what—the cops I know* do *care.*

But then I realize...damn it. I understand the old guy. I understand the woman with the baby. And what I understand is that this whole situation sucks.

"Well, you got your wish tonight," says another woman in the crowd. She's wearing purple eyeglasses and has her hair in curlers.

"Yeah," she says. "The police shot one of the gang members. Blood. Guts. The whole thing. The ambulance just left ten minutes ago, and look, it's already on the news."

Hang on. A police shooting? The woman holds up her cell phone. A television title says, POLICE SHOOTING IN SOUTHEAST. GANG WARS!

Everything inside me shifts. My stomach knots up. My brain has trouble focusing.

"Who was it?" I say. "Did they say if it was a cop in uniform?"

"You know as much as I know," says the woman.

The browser switches to a different piece of news, some new headline about corruption in the Baltimore judicial system. Damn. Is there ever anything good on the news?

Gabe asks, "You sure they didn't mention who..."

The lady with the phone doesn't even let him finish the sentence. She says, "Are you boys listening? Like I said, you know as much as I do."

My stomach knot is only getting tighter.

I tell Gabe that we should leave.

He nods.

I can see that he has the same worry I do: that the cop who fired the gun might have been my dad.

CHAPTER 4

WE ALL CALL her Nana Mama. Fact is, everybody in our family, and even some friends and neighbors, call her Nana Mama.

This truly awesome lady is my dad's grandmother, who lives with us. She's totally unique compared to everyone else I know. Nana Mama can, at the very same time, be the nicest person in the world and the toughest person in the world. If you're expecting some wise old sage spouting wisdom, or some funny old lady, then you definitely have the wrong person. But if you want a woman who's smart and generous, then you have Nana Mama. And that's exactly who I usually want.

Nana and I agree on lots of things. Like I said, she's so smart that it's hard not to come over to her point of view. But not always. I'll show you what I mean.

After last night over at the Stanton Houses I'm hurting from too little sleep, and I need to get some breakfast in me.

Damn. Me and breakfast and Nana Mama. Breakfast is one of those things that we do not see eye-to-eye on. To me the best breakfast is small and sweet, like a bowl of Cocoa Puffs. Maybe a piece of toast with a big smear of peanut butter and a sprinkle of brown sugar. If there's a Hostess donut handy, that'll do, too. For Nana Mama, breakfast is—you probably already guessed—a much bigger deal: waffles and/or griddle cakes, bacon and/or ham steak, eggs and/or cheese grits.

What makes the early morning even tougher is that my great-grandma always seems to have the energy to debate the breakfast issue. I usually do not. I especially do not this morning.

Today I am seriously late for breakfast. Going to bed at after four in the morning is not good prep for getting up at seven. Already Nana has tried two times to rouse me. Then she finally sent my sister up with four ice cubes, which Jannie tossed into my bed. That cruel arctic blast finally got me up, but I'm still running really late. A shower could help me, but I've got to settle for a splash of water on my face.

I walk into the kitchen. All is suspiciously calm. Nana Mama's sipping a cup of tea. Jannie's chomping on a roll with bacon. Hmmm. The whole scene seems too quiet for my own good.

"Well, good morning, young man," says Nana Mama. She gives me a small smile. This is followed by a slight nod. And all this is followed by my sister interjecting annoyingly.

"So nice of you to join us," says Jannie.

I shoot my sister one of my mean faces. Like she cares about my mean faces.

I wait for Nana Mama to start her lecture on a "good breakfast," but instead she points to the box of Cocoa Puffs. She's obviously placed that cereal on the table for my convenience.

Something's not right. But why go looking for trouble? I pour my cereal.

"You sure had a problem getting yourself out of bed today, Ali," Nana says.

"I was tired," I say.

"Were you up late?" Nana asks. There is a tone to her voice that is almost as sweet as my cereal.

"Yes, ma'am."

"Were you rehearsing your class speech?" she asks. Her voice remains careful and slow.

"Yes, I was."

Let's just stop right there for a moment, because here's the problem. First of all, I'm telling a big fat lie, and lying just does not fly in the Cross household. Even worse, it's an especially bad lie, because Nana Mama has a nose for fibbing like a bloodhound for a criminal on the run.

"Well, I'm glad you're working on it so hard," she says. "After all, you told me that the speech is going to be one-quarter of your final grade."

I nod. And I glance over at Jannie. She's watching this little scene as if it were as interesting as the season finale of *The Bachelorette*.

Then Nana says, "Did you practice your speech in front of Bree or your daddy? A little bit of polishing never hurt."

"I should've, but I didn't have time. I finished too late," I say.

Nana nods. But she looks...well, she looks quietly unconcerned. I know I'm about to get caught.

Then, at that moment, like an actor in a movie, my dad walks right in through the kitchen door.

He looks pretty awful, especially for him, a man who thinks it's important to always look "put together."

His eyes are really bloodshot. His white shirt is blotchy with sweat stains. He says, "Morning, everyone," very quietly. It's obvious to all of us that he's just returned from a tough night. But I'm the only one in the family who knows exactly where he's been and what he's been doing.

My phone rings. Everyone pretends they don't hear it, including me. The last thing I need is a lecture on etiquette, which always includes the rule about telephones at the table.

"Everything okay, Alex?" Nana asks.

Dad's voice is flat, serious. "Honestly, everything's *not* okay. Everything is, to put it simply, a nightmare."

"What's going on?" I ask.

He does not answer me immediately. The long pause has me nervous. He's onto something. Finally he speaks.

"We had some problems last night. Problems with a gang. We arrested three of the members. Just over on 18th Street," he says. He shakes his head slowly and sadly and says, "And there was a fourth one. I regret to say that this one ended up getting shot."

We all become completely silent. I get the feeling that Dad is looking at me longer than he should. But I'm not sure. Finally he takes a sip of the coffee that Nana's poured for him.

Me? I'm just scared.

Yeah, I'm scared that he and Nana might figure out—or even already know—that I've told a big lie.

Maybe he saw me. Maybe he texted Nana. But these are small worries.

Because, yeah, I'm really scared that there have been gang fights and a shooting right in our own neighborhood.

But I've got to say that the thing that scares me most is this: that Dad might be in trouble.

CHAPTER 5

I'M DOING MY best to quick-walk to school. My eyes are dry from no sleep. My brain is foggy, but I'm trying to work with it. I should be thinking about my speech, the speech I'm totally unprepared for. But damn it. I can't concentrate. Because I just can't stop thinking about last night.

Two things in particular are messing with me. The first is pretty obvious: I'm really worried that my dad may have been the person who fired the shot, and yet... and the second thing? Well, I've got to admit that the crime scene last night was really exciting, more exciting than anything else lately.

My brain just won't snap into focus. Okay, back to the speech. Not only do I not have a persuasive speech, I don't even have a topic for a persuasive speech.

Hopeless. Dead hopeless. Ms. Townsend gave us some suggestions: "Gender Equality in Sports" and "Take-home Exams versus Classroom Testing" or "Unplugging One Day a Week." But these topics weren't doing it for me. Usually with an assignment I spend a lot of time with my good buddy Doctor Google. But not on this one. I was lost.

Sometimes, I do this thing where I can actually trick myself into coming up with an idea. Here goes. I keep walking and then I start talking out loud.

"Good afternoon, Ms. Townsend and fellow students. . . ." Yeah, I know. I'm sounding particularly ridiculous here. But I'm going to stop and try this again.

"Hello, class, I'm here to talk about a topic that means quite a lot to me. . ." I say to an invisible classroom. Big problem. I don't know what to say next, and what I need to say next is what it is I'm going to speak about. So, as you may have noticed, I am chasing my own tail.

Okay, one more try.

"This is my speech, and I am ready to persuade you that...that...I am here to persuade you...I'm going to try to persuade you...that...that I am... not a total idiot."

Well, that won't work, either. But it might get a laugh.

I give up. It's over. Not happening.

Then I hear a loud and familiar voice. It's my guy Cedric.

"Hey, Ali. We've been following you. Did you know you've been talking to yourself?"

I want to say something like, *Yeah. It sure beats talking to you.* But I'm in no state of mind for a clapback contest.

Cedric is walking with our friend Mateo. I won't say that they honestly look like father and son, even though we're all in the same grade, but they sort of do. You see, for some weird biological reason, Cedric is not only about a foot taller than the rest of us, but he actually *looks* older. He could easily pass for seventeen. And when you're in middle school, looking older is a gift from heaven. The fact that Cedric must weigh about 175 pounds, most of it muscle, bone, and brains—well, let's just say, you're always aware of Cedric when he's in the room.

"Ali, you heard about the shooting last night over in the Stanton Houses, right?" Mateo asks as the three of us walk.

"Of course I heard."

"Was your dad there?" Mateo asks.

"I guess so."

"I heard they shot one of the guys in the gang," Cedric says.

"I wouldn't know," I say.

Mateo jumps on my line. "Yes, you would. Your dad's a detective."

I don't blow up on them, but I get really annoyed. And I don't hold it inside.

"Listen, you guys. My dad doesn't share police business with me. I don't know anything about the shooting. Who it was. Who fired the gun. Nothing."

What follows is what they call "an awkward pause."

Damn. I probably came on a little too strong.

We walk in silence for a few minutes. Then we turn into the schoolyard. It's right then and there that Mateo says, "Can I ask you a question without you getting mad?"

"Yeah, sure," I say. I can tell Mateo's still a little scared I'll blow up. Then he talks.

"Hey, man, I was just wondering...do you think your dad could have been the shooter?"

I'm with friends. I'll say what I think, what I feel, what I hope.

"Honestly, I don't know," I say.

"Okay. I said that I didn't want you to get mad. Sorry, man," Mateo says.

"Yeah, well. That's a fact. I don't know. I just don't know."

Now Cedric jumps in. He sounds serious.

"I just hope the shooter wasn't Mr. Cross," Cedric says.

"That makes two of us," Mateo says.

My turn. "That makes three of us."

Then Cedric says something I'd never even thought of.

"I mean, after all, Ali, this is gang stuff. And gangs almost always retaliate."

CHAPTER 6

LISTEN. THIS ISN'T the first time someone's given me a hard time for being the "detective's son." I've spent a lot of time—especially in the last few years—trying to answer annoying questions about my dad being a cop. Some people in the Southeast area of DC really hate the police. And other people, well, they think that cops walk around like superheroes, able to stop all crime and problems in the neighborhood. A lot of people think that my dad is responsible for anything the police do—good or bad.

Anyway, I always get over it. So we keep on walking, and things get back to normal for the three of us. By the time we actually get to the school we're talking and joking and generally acting like clowns. Clowns who happen to be best friends.

Anyway, I've got some other problems.

Right now I'm still nervous about being totally unprepared for my speech. So the second I pass through the school entrance metal detector and the security guy says, "Go ahead," I take off full speed down the hallway.

I've got to go to the bathroom.

But not for the usual reasons.

The signs all say NO RUNNING IN HALLS. But I don't listen. Not today. I figure that if I can get even a few minutes on my phone to memorize a couple of hard facts on some topic then I can stumble-fumble-mumble my way through the assignment. There are lots of subjects that will cut it with Ms. Townsend.

Should college athletes be financially compensated?

What can we do about lousy nutrition in school lunches?

Is homework really necessary?

The problem is that not only do those topics leave me totally bored, but I know they'll leave Ms. Townsend pretty bored. She's expecting something a little more from me, a little more interesting, or at least a little more unusual.

I'm about to shove open the boys' room door when I hear someone calling me. If it were Cedric or Mateo or Gabe I would have gone on in (and they would have followed me, I'm sure). But this is a girl's voice.

"Ali, hold up!"

I recognize the voice immediately. It's Sienna Williams. She has a voice that I like listening to a lot, and, well—I can't kid myself—Sienna is a girl that I like a lot.

I can't say that Sienna has the same interest in me. In fact, I don't think she has *any* interest in me. I think in her mind, I'm in the "just-a-friend" category. But I also think that with a little bit of effort on my part I might be able to move myself up to a slightly different category. So I'm sure not going to pass up a chance to stop and talk when she's actually calling to me.

"If you need to go on into the bathroom, don't let me stop you," Sienna says.

"Nah. I can wait," I say. Then I realize that this sounds sort of gross.

"You're usually at school earlier." (Sienna knows that? She's actually noticed when I arrive?)

"Yeah, well. Not today," I say.

"Yeah, uh, obviously," she says. But she says this with a little smile, so I know that she's just teasing.

"Sorry, yeah. Obviously."

"I saw you waiting to go through the machine, and you looked sort of pale and nervous. And I thought I'd ask—is everything okay with you?"

Hmm. Let me think about that question. Is everything okay with me? Well, I barely slept last night. I feel like crap. I'm totally unprepared for my speech. And my dad may have shot someone.

"Yeah, everything's great," I say.

"Good."

Then I think that if I want to keep talking to her, I'd better give her more of an answer.

"I am a little nervous about my speech," I say.

"Faker! You're one of those kids who pretends

they didn't have time to study for the test and then aces it."

"I think you might be confusing me with yourself," I say.

And then we're quiet. Really quiet. Clumsy quiet.

"I guess that's it," she says. "See you in class."

I want to say, *Oh, no, that is not* it *at all.* I want to tell her about last night. About how being at the crime scene felt exciting, like I was exactly where I was meant to be. About how worried I am about my dad. About how glad I am that she stopped and talked to me, and so what difference does it make if I mess up my speech?

"Yeah," I say. "See you in class."

CHAPTER 7

I'M LATE, AND I'm never late.

Class has started, and there is no way I'm going to be able to talk my way out of this speech thing. I'm not going to pretend to be sick. I'm not going to say I accidentally deleted the outline on my phone. No. I've got to deal with this. The only problem is I just don't know how. Like Sienna basically said, I'm usually the nerd who's over-prepared.

The class—about thirty of us—sit in our usual U-shaped formation. But Ms. Townsend dug up a wooden podium and put it front and center. Oh, come on.

I like Ms. T, but she is way too enthusiastic about this speech situation. All bright and smiley, she says, "I, for one, am really looking forward to hearing these speeches."

Then I hear Cedric say (to no one in particular), "I, for one, am not."

I'm sure Ms. Townsend hears Cedric, but she doesn't say anything. She's not going to let some wiseass student dial down her enthusiasm.

Ms. Townsend looks down at the index card she's holding. (She's always holding an index card.) "Let's begin with Lily Panarella."

True to form, Lily is sharp and eager and very impressive. That is, if you happen to care about her speech topic, "Eliminating Dress Code Problems with Affordable School Uniforms." She talks about what's good about uniforms (no clothing obsession) and what's bad (no creativity). Honestly, I never thought about uniforms. To me, a uniform is like a Boy Scout uniform or a police uniform or...uh-oh, I'm getting sucked in. I'm going to start thinking about every person and every topic and forget to think about my own speech.

Dan-the-Man Wilkins is next. I'm prepared to hear a lot of environmental speeches today. And Dan-the-Man does not disappoint: "Can We Reverse Climate Change?" Dan starts talking about trees and plant growth, and I am tuning out this one.

Why am I suddenly not paying attention? No surprise here. I'm scared as hell. I'm thinking about my topic...or my non-topic. I'm so nervous I won't have to pretend to be sick. I may throw up for real.

Gabe is looking at me. He mouths the words, *You okay?* I mouth back one: *No.*

Ms. Townsend thanks Dan for his "informative discourse." Then she addresses the class.

"I have our next speaker listed as Carolyn Tubekis." Of course, all heads turn and look at Carolyn. But Carolyn doesn't move. She doesn't stand up. Ms. T continues speaking.

"Carolyn emailed me last night and said that she had not been able to gather all her source material for her speech. She is waiting to interview two members of a local DC amateur dance group, Movement

Access, to figure out whether dancers or athletes work the hardest. So we'll be hearing Carolyn's presentation at our next class."

Groans all around. Most of the kids don't even try to hide their feelings. Someone even loudly says, "Freakin' lucky."

Come to think of it, yeah. It is freakin' lucky.

You mean all I had to do was *ask* Ms. Townsend for an extension?

All I had to do was make up some "academic" excuse?

I know. I know. I can hear Nana Mama: *You mean all you had to do was* lie?

"So, we'll move on," I hear Ms. Townsend say. "Our next speaker..." She looks down at her index card. "Our next speaker will be..."

You guessed it.

CHAPTER 8

THE USUAL SYMPTOMS. Just like a cartoon. Knees weak. Heart racing. Stomach churning. Hands sweating. Arms shaking...no. Wait. Not just my arms. Damn. My whole body is shaking, and it feels like every inch of my skin has been painted with sweat.

It takes me about three weeks to walk from my desk to the podium.

Then, as soon as I reach the podium, Ms. T speaks.

"I don't seem to have your topic listed, Ali. I don't think you ever emailed it to me. So this will be a surprise for all of us."

"For me, too," I say. That line gets a laugh, but I'm the only one who knows that I'm accidentally thinking out loud.

And then there's something like a wild little explosion in my brain. Not precisely a miracle, but as close as I've ever come to a personal phenomenon. My mind turns on a kind of recording, a super-sharp video, a movie that I've never seen before but I'm seeing now. It's a new kind of scene from last night. Not just the three gang members being put in patrol cars, but the crowd. The crowd is angry and disappointed and confused. I see their faces, a series of close-ups. They are watching the crime scene. I am watching them watching the crime scene.

"Whenever you're ready, Ali." Ms. Townsend says.

The class is quiet, strangely quiet. Gabe and Cedric look nervous for me. I glance at Sienna. In that glance, I see a little bit of worry and a little bit of sympathy on her face. Which makes a little butterfly flutter in my stomach.

And then everything suddenly comes together inside my brain! How'd this happen?

It's as if the snatches of conversations I heard from last night's crowd are coming out of my own mouth.

"Crime. Crime. Crime, and even more crime," I say. I'm getting into it. I keep going. "That's what's going on here in Southeast. People getting held up with knives and guns. Old people getting knocked down. Little kids endangered. And where does most of the crime in Southeast come from? The gangs."

Suddenly a rough voice shouts out, "Tell 'em, Cross! Tell 'em loud!"

That voice belongs to A-Train, a guy who likes me sometimes and gives me deep grief other times. Right this moment he's on my side.

Then, all of a sudden, A-Train's girl, Gracie Howard, yells out, "We don't need a church meeting, Ali. Just give your speech."

Gracie is right. For this moment I have the group with me, but I know that drama turns to bull quickly. I'm out for the save. I've got the facts. I give my speech.

"This crime bonanza is happening right here in Southeast DC. Homicides are up 8 percent. Car jackings are up 15 percent. And since you all live right here, you don't need numbers to know that the problem is the gangs. All I'm doing is supplying the statistics."

I know that I am spouting truth. I follow the facts. I eat them up online. I'm tuned in to police messages.

Then I hear, "Solutions, man? Have you got any of those?" This question comes from Gabe. Gabe, of all people. Is my best friend messing with me?

"Yeah, I have some thoughts. But right now I'm just laying out the story," I say. Then I can't help adding, "Thanks for asking, Gabe."

I try to cut more criticism off at the pass. I tell everyone that social services—adolescent counseling, after-school recreation groups, psychotherapy clinics—are more available than ever.

"There has been more money, 25 percent more money, spent on social services this year than was spent in the last three years combined. So what's the problem?"

Suddenly I hear a new voice, a gentler voice, firm but not angry.

"Could it be the police are not doing their jobs? Or maybe doing their jobs but not doing them well enough?"

Damn. That's Sienna talking. It's a punch in the stomach, a kick in the butt. First Gabe. Now her.

Then she adds a quick, "I'm just saying there might be problems with the cops. But Ali is speaking big truth about the gangs and Southeast."

Everyone is quiet now, including Ms. Townsend. I jump right back in.

"I could rattle off some more numbers if you want. But, listen, you live here. So you don't just *know* the facts. You *live* the facts."

Finally Ms. Townsend speaks. I thank her silently; the water here in the deep end of the pool was about to cover my nose.

"First of all, thank you, Ali. Secondly, I want to say that this is exactly what a good speech should do. Inspire. Give us reasons to think and argue. Let's keep the discussion going."

And we do. I'm a little scared, but mostly relieved that I made it this far.

One boy says that the police department is "woefully understaffed." (Where'd that guy dig up the word *woefully*?)

Another girl says, "Southeast always sucked, and there's just no cure."

Luckily, we have to wrap up. Some boy I barely know, José Gonzalez, says he thought my speech was "dynamic and powerful."

Hey, maybe my speech was a success. Unfortunately, this José guy does not start a trend. My on-again-off-again buddy A-Train decides to add something else. This time it's not particularly positive.

"Hey, let's face it," he says. "Ali is always going to be on the side of the police. I mean, come on, his father is a cop."

"That's a load o—" I start to say, and then I think better of it. Instead I just say, "Look, like everyone, I try to be objective about stuff."

"Yeah, you *try* maybe. But are you objective? Can you even be objective? Come on, this is your dad."

All I say is, "Maybe we can pick this up next time, man. For now, I'll just say, 'thanks for listening.' "

Ms. Townsend decides to take over.

"Great speech, Ali. And a great discussion. We'll pick it up next class," she says.

Chapter 9

When I walk home from school my biggest fear is *not* shaking off some drug dealer who's trying to sell me blue caps or horse. And it's almost *never* some tough-guy jerk asking me to "loan" him five bucks. They almost never scare me. (Not because I'm brave, but because I'm fast.)

The only thing I'm really afraid of is what I call "Cell Smash." That's when a few hundred kids walk like zombies on the streets near the school, and almost every single one of those kids is looking down at their phone.

Walk. Walk. Smash!

Walk. Walk. Smash!

"Whoa" and "Watch it, fool" always come too late.

But I'm going to risk being part of the Cell Smash crowd today. I need a news update. And I want it right away, about the gang scene last night. And, of course, about the shooter.

So the second I leave school property I'm punching into Google: "shooting gang fight arrest Southeast DC." The first news listing I read is from the good-old kinda-reliable Washington *Inquirer*.

> **NEW DETAILS IN SOUTHEAST CONFLICT.** New information emerged in last night's gang-related arrests in the Southeast neighborhood. Responding to urgent local appeals, fourteen police officers and detectives intervened in a violent confrontation between two groups known locally as "Nation of Snakes" and "Skull Street." Three arrests were made. More reports as news happens.

I keep looking. I keep googling. The shooting, man. Can we please get to the shooting? I'm busting with nerves. I scroll my way to a different suggestion farther down the page. This is the super-trash website whose name itself is a joke, *The DC Truth.* But I'm in luck. In just a few seconds I'm reading exactly the kind of article I'm looking for. The headline screams THE BULLETS AND THE BLOODBATH. Now, I didn't hear any bullets or see any bloodbath, but when it comes to crime scenes, I'm new to the job. I don't waste any time reading the story.

> What's worse than a brutal gangland battle? A brutal gangland shooting. That's the chaos and madness that erupted between one member of the often trigger-happy DC police force and a member of the terrifying group known as the Skull Street gang. As part of a police attempt to prevent escalating violence between two notorious Southeast gangs, Officer Jeremy Hanson, an officer with only one year of police force experience, shot and wounded Neil Michael Morrissey in his right arm. Morrissey was later reported in "fair" condition at

United Medical Center. A spokesperson for UMC said that young Morrissey's chances for survival were good, although she emphasized that the bullet wound in his shoulder "left him in severe pain."

I feel sorry for anybody who takes a bullet, whether they're a gang member or not.

The guy I'm feeling *really* bad for is this rookie Jeremy Hanson.

But here's what I'm feeling best about: I am so relieved to learn that my dad was not the shooter.

I decide to do a little bit of media temperature-taking. I move over to Twitter, which is spitting out—at breakneck speed—observations on the incident.

@Sylvia_knowsitall "often trigger-happy" **@DCTruth**. Try "ALWAYS trigger-happy" that's the truth. DC cops shoot to kill. I know. They got my daughter who was walking home from a bridal shower. Summer night. Not even 8 pm or dark yet.

@Sen_Lowry_Duetz The Washington police have a job to do, and they do it with intelligence and care. As a Virginia senator, I know that dealing with local gangs is treacherous. I salute the fine men and women of the neighboring police force. Demand a full investigation immediately.

My Twitter feed is filling up way faster than I can scroll.

As I keep reading, I see that there are plenty of extremists on the I-Hate-Gangs side. They're not trash-talking the police, but they're not really helping the cause of the cops, either.

@JumpinJoeNevell That officer shouldve sprayed both gangs with bullets then we'd solve this gang problem

This Jumpin' Joe Nevell's a regular Shakespeare, huh?

Then you got the Tweeters who walk both sides of the line.

@LuckyLyndaJellyfish Underfunding of outreach social systems and psychological treatment, along with ill-tempered ill-trained police. Formula for disaster. How much proof do we need that gangs are the result of bad planning.

And then there are people, like me, who just wish there was a freaking solution.

I click off my phone.

Listen. I am no social media genius. But the one thing all this Twitter talk shows is that this shooting is going to be a red-hot topic.

CHAPTER 10

AND... IT TURNS out that I'm absolutely right about this story turning hot.

In just a few hours, the shooting in Southeast has become one of the biggest issues in Washington, DC, a town where big news is happening every day.

What I never predicted, though, was that the Cross family was about to become a part of this breaking story.

Here's what happens: by seven o'clock, there are

about one hundred people standing and shouting and singing and carrying signs, and *all of that is happening outside our house*! They're standing on the street, on the sidewalk, on our little patch of front lawn. Mostly grown-ups. A few kids. Two or three old people sitting on folding chairs.

Jannie and I stand a few feet away from our dining room window. But we sure have no trouble hearing the crowd outside. And of course we can see the banners and posters. Plus, even from inside our house I can see the anger in the protesters' eyes and the words on the hand-scrawled signs waving in the air.

COPS GET AWAY WITH MURDER!

is the one sign I can't look away from. I'm thinking, *Wait, you guys. This time, nobody was murdered.* But I get the point. At least I sort of do.

I guess you can hear the shouting from everywhere inside our house. Because all of a sudden Nana Mama comes bustling into the dining room. Bree is right behind her.

"Do you think we should be worried, Nana?" asks Jannie.

"No," says Bree. "As long as they stay peaceful."

"Good luck with that," I say.

"No need for sarcasm," says Nana. Then she says to Bree, "Have you talked to Alex yet?"

"I texted him. He's down at the precinct. He's coming home right now."

"Good," I say.

Just then Jannie says, "Hey, everyone, look on over to the left. They've even got a sign about the cop who—"

"The word is not *cop*. The correct word is *officer*," Bree says.

Respect. In my house, so much is about respect.

"Okay, the *officer* who did the shooting," says Jannie.

ARREST JEREMY HANSON!

Maybe Bree has no trouble staying calm, but I'm getting scared as hell. Some weird rock music is blaring from somewhere in the crowd. Signs are waving in the air. The street is filled with loud voices, harsh music, and people wearing T-shirts that say things like:

TOO MANY COPS
TOO LITTLE JUSTICE

Yeah, I've got to admit it: I'm scared as a little baby.

One group chants "FIRE THE COPS—WHEN?" Another loud group answers, "FIRE THE COPS NOW!"

(I guess no one told 'em that you're supposed to call them "officers.")

These two groups go back and forth with their chanting, over and over and over again. Meanwhile Nana Mama walks right up close to the dining room window and carefully surveys the scene. Her nose is almost touching the glass.

Okay, I know you can't have lived in Southeast and not seen demonstrations and protests and screaming crowds. But it's something I don't think I'll ever get used to. And right now, with this crowd,

I'm scared for Nana Mama. I'm scared for all of us Crosses.

Nana Mama looks away from the angry crowd. She turns and speaks to Bree.

"Did Alex tell us what we should do?"

"He only said not to worry, and that all of us should stay inside until he gets home."

"Yes, ma'am. Well, that's one opinion," says Nana. Then she unties her apron, folds it neatly, and places it on the dining table.

She walks from the dining room to our little front hall. She opens the front door and steps out on the brick stoop and stands facing the crowd.

"Fire the cops!"

"When?"

"Fire the cops now!"

"Fire the cops!"

"When?"

"Fire the cops now!"

The chanting is not going to stop for anyone, not even Nana Mama.

Chapter 11

"**Good evening, everybody.** Welcome. Welcome to my *home*. Yes. My *home*. I call it that because my family and I live here."

I am always amazed at how strong Nana Mama's voice is. Today she sounds even stronger than usual. Plus, her voice is remarkably calm. I can only imagine that if I had to step out in front of a crowd like this...well, never mind.

Plenty of the protesters actually know Nana Mama. I mean, man, she was a schoolteacher in this neighborhood for sixty-five years. Sixty-five years! That means that there are people out there who had her as a teacher, whose children had her, whose grandchildren had her.

She is one brave and determined lady. As I watch her, I figure that if Nana Mama can face the crowd, I can dig up a spoonful of courage, too. I join Nana Mama on the stoop. I'm hoping that this crowd will quiet down, show a little respect for this local legend. But this bunch is riled up. They're not mean-looking, but they look...well, they look determined. It's old people and young people. I recognize three or four guys from school, including A-Train and Cedric's older brother, Anthony. And then my heart jumps, a sad sort of jump. I see my favorite girl, Sienna. She is standing with her mother and father.

Nana Mama tries again. She takes a deep breath and tries again.

"I'll wait for you all," she says. "Somebody tell me when I can talk."

There's a noticeable decrease in the shouting, but it's still not nearly quiet enough for Nana to be heard.

So she waits. She looks straight ahead. She's not moving. As for me, I'm still staring at Sienna, hoping that she looks back at me. If we make eye contact, at least that would be something. I wonder what side she's on. If she's standing outside my house because she's protesting my family.

A few feet away from where I'm standing is a tough-looking guy wearing a black sleeveless shirt that says on it: POLICE THE POLICE. I don't know where my own voice suddenly comes from, but I lean in and talk to this dude.

"Hey, man," I say. "Could you pass the word on to quiet 'em all down? My Nana has something to say."

At first I think the guy is going to tell me to do something nasty to myself. Instead he nods and turns to two women behind him. In a really loud voice, the guy says: "Quiet down. Pass it on." And it works. Well, it sort of works. More people speak to the people behind them. "Quiet down. Pass it on." "Let the old lady talk." "Quiet, everyone."

The talking and shouting and chanting don't completely stop. But there's some real decrease in the noise level. It sorta sounds like just a big group of people waiting for a Wizards home game to start.

After a few minutes the guy in the sleeveless shirt looks at me and says, "Tell the old lady to talk. It's not going to get any quieter than this."

"I heard him," Nana says. And she starts to speak.

"I don't have a lot to say..." she begins.

But before she can utter another word, a voice from the crowd yells, "Where's Alex Cross?"

This shout is followed by another: "This is Alex Cross's house. We want to hear from Alex Cross."

Nana wastes no time in responding.

"This is *my* house. So you're going to hear from me."

She pauses for a moment, just a moment. I think that both of us understand that the crowd could get loud again quickly.

"I understand your anger. But I'm telling you this—it's something I learned because I've lived so long. And here it is: we all need one another. Life has to be in balance. Do you understand that? This neighborhood—your neighborhood, my neighborhood—it just cannot survive without the police. So we all have to do better.

Yes, and that means the police, too. And, yes, every person in the neighborhood. And..."

Suddenly, there is some scattered booing in the crowd.

"Go ahead. Boo all you want. Do whatever you want. Those are your rights! Boo! Cheer! That's the freedom that'll save us," Nana says.

And just as suddenly, there is a smattering of cheers. It's not a lot, but it's something. Nana Mama smiles. Gotta hand it to her. Maybe it's from teaching thousands of kids over the years. But this lady sure knows how to handle a crowd.

CHAPTER 12

I ALWAYS THOUGHT this whole gang dispute and police shooting was going to turn into a big deal. But I never dreamed it would turn out to be this big.

The morning after the demonstration, I wake up to a phone call from Cedric. The time? Exactly five a.m. And the fact that it's an actual phone call and not a text message tells me that it's something important.

He starts talking before I say a word.

"Hey, man. What's happening with you? Are you trying to get yourself in trouble?"

"What are you talking about?" I ask.

"I'm talking about this new Instagram account of yours. What is this @AliCross4Cops junk?" (Only, Cedric doesn't use the word *junk*.)

I open the app and search for it.

Oh, damn! It's not what Cedric thinks it is. It isn't my account at all. Somebody has made a whole new account just to troll me—with my face staring back in the profile picture and everything. I start scrolling through @AliCross4Cops and see maybe thirty or forty photos of cops—cops in groups, cops in uniform, cops arresting people, cops with their guns drawn, all of the cops looking mean, angry. Even the cops with little kids. Even the cops at shelters during Christmas. Every one of them looks mean, some even downright vicious.

Oh, yeah, and there's a special touch. Each and every police photo is totally decorated with that corny heart emoji. ♥

And the worst thing of all.

The most recent photo on the Instagram page

is a screenshot of Keanu Reeves from a John Wick movie, holding a machine gun. Only instead of Keanu's head they've photoshopped on a different head—my dad's. Alex Cross holding a machine gun!

"This junk isn't mine, Cede," I say. (Only, I don't use the word *junk*, either.)

"Somebody's gone and set up a fake," Cedric says.

I am now wildly wide awake. My eyes are burning and my hands are sweating.

I scour Twitter and Instagram as fast as I can. It's like I'm playing an out-of-control electric keyboard.

In the next few hours, a gigantic pile of text messages comes streaming in.

Here's a mild one.

Guess we know 4 sure whose side ur on, Ali

Here's an extreme one.

Next time they shoot I hope they shoot you

And, oh, my God. Here's one from Sienna.

If this is legit I'm disappointed.

Chapter 13

Look. It's never been a picnic being a detective's kid. But now it's really starting to hurt. Wild posts on Instagram. Outrageous stuff on Twitter. Come on, everybody. In case you haven't heard: I am not responsible for the entire DC police department. I am also not responsible for people creating phantom accounts under my name. It's a freaking mess. A mess that is totally out of my control.

That morning at school things are no better. In fact everything is pure hell.

Okay, my usual crew, Cedric and Mateo, are there for me.

"Ignore the jerks, Ali," Mateo says when I run into him just outside of school.

"Easy for you, Mat-so," I say. And just like in a cheesy sitcom, Larry Ross and his super pretty girlfriend, Megan, pass in front of us. With all the fake over-the-top drama he can muster, Larry yells out, "Don't shoot, officer. Please. Don't shoot!"

Megan apparently thinks her boyfriend is hilarious. She is cracking up laughing, so Larry continues with his little routine, "Let's get out of here, babe. I don't want us to get hurt. You know these out-of-control cops!"

They both laugh and run. Mateo speaks.

"Like I said, Ali. Ignore the jerks. And ignore their girlfriends, too."

"And like *I* said, that's easy for you to say."

At least Larry and Megan were *trying* to be funny. They didn't succeed, but maybe they were just having fun. Same goes for the two girls behind me in the line for the metal detector. One of them calls me *Officer* Cross. The other one says with a laugh,

"Where's your police uniform, Ali? I love a man in uniform."

But not everyone is trying to work funny. One guy whom I don't even know follows me into the bathroom. He watches me while I use the facilities. When I go to wash my hands, the guy parks at the sink next to me, standing too close and watching me with way too much interest.

His face is mean. He spits into the sink and speaks to me in a squeaky-weird voice that scares the hell out of me.

"You'd better watch yourself, cop kid," he says. He spits again, and he sure doesn't rinse out the porcelain sink before he leaves.

In my first class, math (already not my favorite start to the day), some kids act friendly. They send a small smile or a brief nod in my direction. Cedric passes my desk and says, "Stay cool." I nod. Then he adds, "Talk later."

Class starts. Mr. Gates, a guy who doesn't look much older than some of the kids in the class, is determined to get us to understand cube roots and square roots. I pretty much already understand those two math concepts, and that's good because my mind is not on what Mr. Gates is saying.

My mind is on me and this whole ugly situation.

Okay. I'm feeling sort of sorry for myself. But why not? Hey, I'm thinking I have every right to feel the way I feel. I've been pushed around before because my father is on the force. I even had to hang out with a girl because her mother was a decorated police officer. But it wasn't much of a friendship. That girl and I had nothing to talk about except what a pain it could be to have a police officer for a parent.

I get through math class without being called on, and I start looking for Cedric on my way out of the classroom.

But this is only forty-five minutes into my school day. Out in the hallway somebody bumps into me. It's a hard bump. I lose my balance, but I catch myself, and I don't fall. It's not unusual for this kind of bump to happen in the chaos of changing classes. But because of my current unpopularity, I'm feeling that this bump may not have been particularly "accidental." I look behind me and see that the guy who knocked into me is Darius Dorsey—a funny guy, a pretty nice guy, and also...well, a pretty big guy.

"Hey, D. You got to watch your driving," I say. I try to be light and friendly about it.

"And you got to watch *yourself,* Cross," Darius says. He's not smiling. He looks serious. Not scary. More like grim. He keeps talking.

"You and I are good with each other, right?" he says.

"Yeah, sure," I say.

"Then, here's a little intel I got for you. I suggest you pay attention."

"Yeah, give it to me," I say. I'm only a little nervous.

"Some kids in this school are saying that you're against your own kind of people. That cops come first, and your people come second."

I'm not happy. But I'm not quite angry yet.

"Darius, tell me something I don't already know. That's what some fools think. I'm on everybody's side. And I'm on nobody's side."

"I know that, but not everyone else knows that.

They say because your dad is a detective that you betray your people, that you..."

I cut him off.

"I know what people say, Darius. I've got to go."

"Just trying to help. Take care of yourself. *And* think about standing up with your people."

"Yeah, sure. Thanks." I start walking away. I've already decided that I'm going to be late for my next class. In fact, I'm actually going to skip it, which is pretty radical for me. Okay, the class is Spanish, so it won't be *that* radical. I can catch up with an online lesson. I've got to sit still for a few minutes and get my brain together.

I'm not angry. I'm not scared. But what the hell am I feeling?

The warning buzzer rings for the next period. *Adios,* Spanish class.

Then it hits me. I know what I'm feeling.

I'm alone. I'm just caught in this whole big thing—the policeman's son versus the police versus everyone else and their opinions—alone.

I try thinking through it, but I don't even have the energy to do that.

I sit in the stairwell and watch a few kids try to get to class before they rack up three tardy slips and have to go to breakfast club.

I watch Sienna rushing up the stairs three steps at a time. And honestly, I'm so down that I don't even feel better when she shoots a nod in my direction. I'm a little surprised that Sienna even acknowledges me.

As she disappears, three guys—one of them is A-Train—come strolling along. They're going to be late for their next class, and it's pretty clear that none of them really care.

"Hey, Cross. You skipping class?" says A-Train. I'm not liking his tone of voice.

"Best be careful, Cross," says one of the guys with him. "I heard they've got a new punishment for kids who show up late for class."

"Right on, Ronnie. New rule is: If you're late, even once, they shoot you. They don't kill you. But they do shoot you."

All three of them crack themselves up.

I stand up fast.

"You guys are fools. Not even funny fools. Just plain old fools!" I yell.

What am I saying? What am I doing? Am I nuts? Three of them. And one of them is A-Train. I shouldn't even think about messing with them. I backtrack.

All I say is, "Leave me alone, huh? Just leave me alone."

To my complete surprise, that's what they do.

CHAPTER 14

YEAH, TRY SLEEPING, Ali. Just go ahead and try.

I'm listening to some podcast put out by a police training academy in Northbrook, Illinois. The instructor is talking about disarming underage assailants. He's pretty sharp, and he's pretty funny. (Although I've heard my dad say, "Police officers are good at many things. Humor is not one of them.") But then at some point he says, "The first order of business is to make certain that the firearm the assailant is holding is actually a firearm."

And then he just moves on like that's that. Give me a break. Like a cop has *always* made certain before reacting. Maybe this guy is not as sharp as I thought.

I tap off the podcast and tap on a playlist Cedric sent me a few days ago. Cedric is always pushing tunes from groups I've usually never heard of, and if I have heard of them, I really hate them—Neon Trees or Rixton, for example.

I've told Cedric that his faves always sound like stuff from the eighties, stuff that my dad and Bree like. But I appreciate Cedric trying to change me. I've gotta keep an open mind. Or in the case of Cedric's playlist, an open ear. I listen to two tracks, and that's enough. I remove my AirPods. I've got to try to get some sleep.

But five minutes later it looks like that's not going to happen. Because...

Gabe's police scanner app suddenly comes to life, pelting my ears with *ping*s and *ding*s. These ears of mine are working overtime tonight.

Within a second I am reading snippets of Washington, DC, police chatter. There's been a break-in at one of the fancied-up refurbished town houses just off Massachusetts Avenue on 15th Street. They've been trying to "gentrify" this area ever since I can remember. And it looks like the gentrification is not completely catching on. Breaking and entering has actually gone up in the past year. Okay, only by 4 percent. But an increase in crime is never a great statistic.

I don't think it's worth the risk of sneaking out of the house just for a B&E. But then I keep reading.

"The husband and wife owner-residents were restrained with electrical tape; both victims sustained non-life-threatening injuries; elderly resident, female owner's mother, is still unaccounted for."

Elderly? Unaccounted for?

Hey, this could be the police scene I've been hoping for. I can lend my brain, and maybe I can even lend a hand.

I'm out of bed! I'm on my way!

CHAPTER 15

IT TAKES ME ten minutes to get from my house to the crime scene. It would have taken eight minutes, except I had to be really quiet sneaking out, careful not to wake Jannie or Bree or Dad or especially Nana Mama, who is able to hear a pin drop even if the pin is dropping in a house that's three blocks away.

When I get to the house on 15th Street, I'm immediately hit with a few surprises.

First surprise: Turns out that the old lady, the

mother of the woman who'd been tied up with her husband, is no longer missing. Cedric, who's standing there with Gabe, tells me that they found the old lady hiding in a big, creaky wooden trunk in the basement. Of course I'm glad that they found her safe and everything, but a little piece of me, I'm ashamed to say, was hoping for some real crime drama.

Oh, yeah, here's my second surprise: Cedric is there! And he's acting like he's always been part of the private, secret little detective unit that Gabe and I started.

I give Gabe a *What the hell is this guy doing here?* look, and Gabe, with just a little shrug and a head tilt, manages to communicate *I'm sorry that I shot off my big mouth and told Cedric, but what's the big deal?*

Okay. Cedric is a friend. Moving on.

This crowd is not nearly as big as the crowd that showed up at the gang fight, but it's big enough. Even though robberies, breaking and entering, and assault are pretty regular events in Southeast, this group—maybe it's thirty people—seems angrier than the last.

I study this new crowd. Maybe I'll see some familiar faces from the demonstration outside our own house. No. No one I know, not even Sienna. Not even—talk about a major relief—Alex Cross. But I can't totally relax. I've got to be on constant lookout for the big man. I know from experience that it would be highly likely for my dad to get a call and get on over to a crime scene, even though when I left my house he and Bree were safely in dreamland.

I watch everything and everyone closely. I watch the young woman, who I'm guessing is the young wife, the person who was tied up. She starts hugging and kissing the old lady. Yeah, they are clearly mother and daughter. The scene is pretty touching to witness. Even for a wannabe tough guy like me.

Four police officers, three plainclothes detectives, emergency rescue people. They're walking around the small front yard. The police move in and out of the house. Two of them keep the small crowd at a distance. I snap some pics of the situation.

Now I'm itching to mingle, talk to the crowd. I can't help myself. I have automatically switched into full detective mode. Yeah. I'll talk to the crowd. Take their temperature. Ask a few questions.

"You live around here, ma'am?" I say to one lady who's wearing a track suit and holding a plastic water bottle.

"Yes, I do," she says. "So what? Why d'you want to know?" She sounds mighty impatient with my simple question. I shift into my sweetest tone.

"I live around here, too," I say. "I was just wondering if you saw anything."

"I didn't see anything." She shakes her head in angry disbelief. "I'm mad and I'm tired of this stuff happening. I've lived here for five years. Things were getting better. Now it's worse than ever."

"Domestic break-ins are only up fractionally," I say, and immediately realize that I sound like a robot.

My interviewee seems to think so, too.

"Fractionally? Fractionally, my butt. This neighborhood is going down and down and down. I got mugged for my cell phone last week coming out of the Metro. I reported it. Cops didn't care...."

She keeps talking, but at the magic phrase, "cops didn't care," I brace myself for the chain reaction.

Sure enough. This inspires another woman, same age, to say, "Cops never care. Burglars come into your house when you're at work. They take your electronics and the jewelry that you didn't hide. Hell, they'd take your refrigerator and couch if they had the time."

This lady is not happy. But I'll tell you who is happy: Gabe and Cedric. They're enjoying the fact that I'm getting lectured to.

I turn to yet a third woman, same talkative type I'm guessing.

"Ma'am, what do you think about all this?"

She is calm, thoughtful-sounding in the way she talks.

"I think that the cops do try. I think that most of them care a lot. But there are simply not enough of them."

Uh-oh. Some fierce disagreement here.

"They try? They try?" says the first woman, loudly. "They try when they feel like you're a danger, without getting the full picture. They try when..."

The calmer woman continues. She is calm. You might even call her stern.

"Yes, lady. You heard me right. The police do try. They're not perfect, but the ones I know and see are good men and women. Try living in Southeast without 'em."

I glance at Gabe and Cedric. Both my friends are listening kinda seriously.

I'm listening seriously, too. This is the same, identical debate that's churning up my life at school. Only at school, it's just a debate. Right here? This is real life.

CHAPTER 16

IT WAS BOUND to happen.

I just didn't think it was going to happen so soon.

I've been on two cases since Gabe set up my maybe-illegal police-radio app. Never woke up the family. Made it to and from the crime scenes safe and sound. Got home just fine. And now, all of a sudden...BUSTED! No. No. I don't get busted by the police or anything. But maybe I would've been better off if they *had* busted me instead of the person who does. Let me explain.

I unlock the door to the kitchen quick and quiet. Not a click or a tumble or a squeak. I carefully relatch and relock and then...

"Welcome home, Ali. Who might you have been visiting at three forty-five in the morning?"

Nana Mama, of course. She's sitting at the kitchen table with a cup of something steaming in front of her, probably her favorite beverage, boiled water with lemon and sugar and "a pinch of turmeric." Her voice is surprisingly calm. She's got me, but maybe she'll cut me a break.

"Explain yourself, young man."

"I knew it was late, Nana. But I didn't know it was that late."

How foolish can I be? I didn't know the time? That's not gonna fly with Nana.

"Ali, let's not do some old comedy routine. You know what I mean, where I ask you a completely reasonable question and you snap back with a lie."

"Yes, ma'am," I say.

"Right," she says. "So, answer the question. Where've you been?"

I stammer and sputter a little. But then I figure that the faster I answer, the safer I'll be. I don't know. I think it'll sound more truthful that way. And I do plan on telling the truth.

"My friend Gabe told me that there was a police investigation over near Massachusetts Avenue and 15th Street. So I went over there to meet up with him, see what was going on."

I guess I overcooked the truth just enough that Nana Mama wrinkles her forehead and asks another question, a "follow-up for clarification," she calls it.

"How did Gabe learn about a police investigation at three in the morning? Did he recently join the DC force?"

"Well, he just knew," I say.

"He just knew," she repeats. Nana Mama has had enough. She is ready to give her closing summation and argument.

"I don't know what you're up to, Ali. And it's not because I don't care. I care a great deal. But I'm not in the mood to launch a full-scale interview right now. However, I do have this to say. You know what this neighborhood is like at three forty-five in the morning. You know how dangerous it can be. I don't *know* how you and your friend 'just *know*' what's happening on the street when you should be sleeping or praying in your bed."

Obviously, I'm not about to tell her about my awesome new cell phone setup. And, of course, I don't tell her how the crime scenes hypnotize me. Or about...

"Are you listening?" she asks.

"Yes, Nana."

Then she says something that brings me an instant wave of relief.

"I will not share this information with your father, but..."

"Thanks, Nana," I say.

"Hold on," she says. "You may have noticed that I used the word *but*. So I will not, on this one occasion, share this story with your father, *BUT* if it ever happens again, I will not waste any time getting it to him."

I decide it'd be best not to say anything except,

"Thank you, Nana." And I've got to admit that I am truly thankful.

"Ali, take care of yourself. Watch out for yourself. Be a man."

I'm a little confused. Be a man?

Isn't that what I'm trying to do?

Chapter 17

Whenever there's a serious (and let's just say "potentially dangerous") disagreement about something in my school, the battles seem to take place in some very specific places—the boys' locker room, the girls' locker room, the small scruffy patch of weeds behind the handball court where kids go to smoke. But the place where the most serious confrontations take place is almost always the school cafeteria. I know. From experience.

In the past few days, the arguments over the

police situation have calmed down a little. But this thing is not going away fast. In the week since the shooting, most kids have broken off into four groups.

The first group thinks that the whole system is broken and that almost all cops abuse their power. The second group thinks that almost all cops are brave, kind, decent men and women who faithfully guard the community. Then there is a third group of kids who really don't have an opinion and, to quote my bud Cedric, "care mainly about basketball, clothes, and where they're going to hang out on Friday night." Finally, there is a fourth group, and that group is mainly made up of...well, I think I'm actually the only member of that group. I'm the only one who kind of thinks that I could sometimes be a member of any of the other three groups. That's how complicated the situation is. At least to me.

The real truth is that I'm sick and tired and angry at having to take abuse from some of the kids in the first group. This is the group who loud-whispered "cop kid" when they passed me by. I was also sure that someone in this group had Scotch-taped two strips of raw bacon to my locker. (Bacon. Pig. Cops are pigs. Get it? Freaking hilarious, no?)

Anyway, around this time, a week after the shooting incident, I'm sitting at a cafeteria table with Cedric (mac and cheese, bag of chips), Mateo (salad with way too much blue cheese dressing, two apples, Little Debbie coffee cake), and these two girls I sorta know, Ava and her girlfriend Deidre (they're sharing a large order of fries and two Cokes that they snuck in). I'm about to dive into the tuna on whole wheat toast that Nana Mama packed for me. Then, just like I'm in a prank TikTok video, I've got my mouth wide open, the sandwich about to enter, and just before my teeth chomp down, out of the corner of my eye, I see two guys and a girl standing right at my shoulder.

I've never seen these three kids before. It's easy to figure out that they're older than me and my friends. Maybe they're a couple years older, maybe even from the high school.

"You're Ali Cross?" the bigger of the two guys asks me.

The guy doesn't sound tough or mean. In fact, he's pretty soft-spoken. Even so, I decide I'd be better off standing up. I think I read somewhere that it's always safer to be on eye level with someone who might give you trouble.

"Yeah, I'm Ali," I say. "What's up?"

The second guy talks.

"You're the cop kid?" He's nowhere near as soft-spoken as the first guy.

"So that's what this is about?" I ask.

I'd better stop right here and tell you the truth. I am scared as hell.

Like I said, these guys are big, not super-big, but big enough, two or three school years bigger than me, if you know what I mean.

"Let me explain something, tiny man," says the first guy, this time loudly. (He calls me "tiny man." This is not a good sign. So much for being soft-spoken.)

I'm still scared as hell, but for some reason I'm not *more* scared, which I guess I should be.

It could be that, standing up, I see that realistically he's only about one or two inches taller than me. The weight difference between us? Not much. We're both pretty scrawny.

But even with all that, and even with a year of good judo lessons, and...oh, who am I kidding? I can't take these guys. As for Cedric and Mateo...like I said, who am I kidding? All three of us couldn't take these guys on.

And anyway, the last thing I want is a fight.

Then the first guy says, "I want to introduce myself. I'm Jayden Walker."

The name means nothing to me.

Then he adds, "I'm Grady Walker's older brother."

This is bad. Really, really bad.

The name Grady Walker does mean something to me. In fact, it means a lot to most people I know.

Grady Walker was a seventh-grade boy from Southeast who was climbing through the front porch window of his mother's house two years ago. The TV inside the house was so loud that it's likely that Grady did not hear the officer yell "Stop." The officer says that he yelled "Stop" twice.

Yeah, you can guess the really bad rest of the story. The officer shot once. Grady died.

It was awful. Maybe the worst thing I ever heard about in my very bad neighborhood. There was heartbreak. There was anger. And we all found out fast that heartbreak and anger are not a fine mixture. There were protests and memorial services and rivers of tears.

Turns out that the officer who shot Grady was Black. But that didn't make any difference. Grady was shot by a cop. Grady was dead.

I say, "I knew your brother. Not well. But I knew him. He was a good kid. I mean that. I'm sorry for your loss."

I hold my hand in the air, expecting Jayden Walker to hold up his own hand and slap it against mine. He does not.

Jayden and I just stare at each other. Then I look away and I see that a small crowd has assembled right around us. I mean: this is cafeteria prime time. A possible fight. Go ahead, let your pizza slice get cold. Ladies and gentlemen, we've got a sold-out stadium here today.

For the first time, the female member of this trio speaks. Her voice is strong, serious.

"Look, man. We're talkin' about Jayden's little brother. Maybe you don't understand. So, I can do the explaining you need. We heard that you're going around defending cops. And Jayden and his group have had a project going on for about two years. They are trying to get this town to understand that the cops are nothing but a pack of killers. Killers. You understand that?"

I am both confused and angry. Why do two such different emotions always seem to show up at the same time?

"I'm not 'defending' cops," I say. "I'm just trying to bring some kind of common sense to the situation."

Jayden's eyes narrow. "Here's some common sense. My little bro is dead because some cop put a bullet in him."

The amazing thing is this: I understand exactly how Jayden feels. But here's the other thing: my dad is a cop. And my dad is a good man. I know that he'd feel horribly if it'd been him that killed Grady. I understand that I feel safer with him around. But, oh, man, this is not the time or place to try to deliver that lecture.

In the next second or two Jayden grabs me hard by my shoulders. He holds me, and I'm thinking—again, in the span of that same second or two—that if this guy takes a swing at me, I'm toast. Maybe I could shake him off after a couple blows and run away. But if I can't, if I've got to stay here and fight, I know I don't have a chance.

How did I end up here? In this situation? How did this whole thing grow so big, so fast? And how the hell do I end it? Stop it? Fix it?

But there's no way I can figure it out now.

"Break it up! Break it up!" I hear. The voice is very loud, forceful. And everybody recognizes it. It's the familiar voice of Coach Hassim. From the crowd come a few weak shouts of "Fight! Let 'em fight."

And it is just at that moment, the moment the coach yells his last "Break it up," that I bring both my arms up—as hard as I can—to break myself free from Jayden's grip on my shoulders. Then I give Jayden a weak shove, not actually in anger, just to get myself away from him. Jayden stumbles backward. Not a big stumble. He gets himself together really quickly. But this all occurs at the precise moment that Coach Hassim is sizing up the scene.

Of course it clearly looks like I'm the one who was looking for a fight.

Coach recognizes Jayden and his friends. He tells them to go on back to their own school. Then he tells me to follow him to his office. What'll happen to me? Demerits? Detention? Breakfast club? A stern talking-to?

Whatever. It can't be as lousy as what happens next. As Coach Hassim and I walk through the suddenly quiet cafeteria, all eyes are on us. One of those pairs of eyes belongs to Sienna. I see her. She is looking right at me. I give her a small smile. But she just frowns and shakes her head and then looks away.

CHAPTER 18

IT SEEMS LIKE the subject of gangs has become the most important thing in my life. It wasn't always that way for me, but I gotta say that it's always been important to my dad and the people he works with.

Grown-ups have a lot to say about gangs. And my dad sure is one of those grown-ups. He's always saying how serious the issue is, how if you could get the gangs under control then we'd improve the city 100 percent. Whatever—the topic has not cooled down. And this shooting has made it hotter than ever... with everybody.

Of course, as we know, I've got some very specific concerns about the gang shooting at the Stanton Houses. Namely, did my father see me at the gang shooting? Did he hear me sneak out to meet Gabe that night?

I've also been starting to wonder, did he hear Nana Mama and me talking when *she* caught me sneaking back in? Did somebody from the school call my dad and tell him about the scene in the cafeteria?

I've been waiting for one of these possibilities. And if Dad does find out about what's been going on, it might mean an Ali-and-father conversation will follow. Or not follow. Or... listen, he is a solid dad. And a fair person. Like he says, "I am a reasonably reasonable person." But I know from experience that he is also a little awkward at man-to-man, father-to-son conversations.

Don't get me wrong; we talk. We talk a lot. But it's usually about easy stuff like basketball and funny stuff that happened at school or in the neighborhood. Sometimes we'll talk about my friends (he's cool with most of them). Sometimes I'll ask him a question, and he'll give me short, simple opinions. If I don't agree with his short, simple opinions, he'll say, "Well, that's what I think, and you shouldn't have asked my opinion if you didn't want it."

Not mean or angry or anything. Usually just with a shrug.

Anyway, since we're not that big on planned sit-down conversations, I'm surprised (and a little freaked) when, after supper tonight, my dad says, "Ali, I could use a cold glass of milk to help wash down Nana's chicken. Pour me a tall one and bring it into the living room, if you please. Get yourself a glass, too, if you want one."

Hmmm? No nasty note to his voice. No drama. Nothing threatening. But if I had to guess, my gut is telling me that he's heard about what went down in the cafeteria today. He probably got a phone call from Coach Hassim or even Ms. Garrity, the assistant principal.

I pour the milk and bring it into the living room.

"Hey, you even remembered to put an ice cube in it," he says with a smile.

"I know you like it that way, ice cold," I say.

"Your mama always thought I was foolish to put ice in milk. She said the ice would melt, but I always told her..."

I finish the sentence. "You always told her it doesn't water down the milk if you drink the milk real fast."

"Precisely," he says, and I figure that maybe this sweet memory of my mom is just a detour for him. Maybe he's having second thoughts about lecturing me about something.

But maybe not. He keeps on talking.

"You know, Ali, you and I have yet to discuss the shooting in the Stanton projects," he says. "And I've discussed it with just about every other person I know. People on the force. Nana. Detective Sampson. Even Jannie. Yet you and I have avoided the subject."

Okay. He knows. I know he knows, and he knows I know he knows. He also...I finally jump in. Simple. Straightforward. This will be my smartest move.

"You saw me there, didn't you?" I ask.

Pause.

"Yes, I did. But that's not what I wanted to discuss," he says.

I keep talking anyway.

"Listen, Dad. I know I shouldn't have been there," I say, a little louder than I need to.

He holds the palm of his hand up, as if to say, *Calm down. I'll do the talking.*

"You understand, Ali, that you were seriously wrong to be there. You're aware of that. So there's no point in carrying on about it. I'll only ask of you one thing: Please don't do something irresponsible and dangerous like that ever again."

I guess a better kid would admit that I'd already done something "irresponsible and dangerous" for a second time, or try to explain why I was at the projects in the first place. But, damn, I'm just not that better kid. Maybe someday I'd own up to it, but this wasn't the day.

Now, Dad moves on to the meat of the discussion.

"Here's what I really want to talk about. I want to hear what you think about the shooting itself, about that young man who was almost killed."

I don't know why, but his question—serious, very somber—shakes me up a little. When in doubt, tell the truth. And that's what I do. Besides, I want him to know a little of what I've been going through.

"I'm not sure what I think. I mean, this 'young man' was part of a gang. He was part of the break-in. This is a bad person."

"Yes. He was certainly no model citizen. But what if the boy had been shot dead?" Dad asks.

"But he wasn't," I say.

"But he could have been."

I pause for a moment. Dad raises his eyebrows.

Then he speaks.

"It's a big problem. A very confusing problem. And it's particularly confusing for those kids who have folks in police work, Ali."

Then I say exactly what I'm thinking.

"Yeah, I oughta know. I'm one of those kids."

"And I'm sure it's tough on you," he says. "Fortunately, you're smart enough, and even man enough, to understand the—let's say—*dimensions* of the problem."

Man enough. Dimensions. I guess he thinks I have the brains and the guts to deal with this. But maybe I don't; should I tell him that?

He finishes drinking his milk. (The ice cube doesn't look any smaller than when I brought the glass to him.)

It turns out that he's not quite finished with me—even though I'm not sure what else to say. He puts down the glass and talks.

"You've met my friend Chris, the deputy officer for off-duty conduct. You may remember that Chris is from Denmark. He spent ten years on the police force over there in Copenhagen. Anyway, Chris once said to me that the biggest difference between the way folks from America think, compared to the way folks from Europe think, is this: in Europe people try to accept the way things happen, the way things are, the things that probably cannot change.

"But in America, well, Americans always think that bad things can change, that if you think hard enough, if you try hard enough, you absolutely can come up with a solution."

He pauses. I think he's waiting for his words to make their way through my mind. But my mind is feeling pretty mixed up.

Then he says, "What do you think about Chris's opinion on the difference between America and Europe and changing things around?"

I look down at the floor. I shuffle my feet. I'm not sure how to answer, so to buy some time I say, "No, Dad. You go first. What do *you* think?"

"What do I think?" he asks. Then he laughs and says, "I'm an American. So, now it's your turn. Tell me. What do you think?"

The truth is, I don't know *what* I think. It's not that simple. Sure, there's plenty of bad stuff in the world you just have to accept. But a lot of other bad stuff, I think, *can* be changed. I think it *has* to be. Does that make me American or European? I'm not sure. I can't figure out an answer to this any more than I can figure out an answer to the police dilemma, and right now, it's definitely making me fed up.

"Here's what I think, Dad. I think you look pretty ridiculous with a milk mustache."

My dad smiles, then seems like he wants to say more. I don't let him.

"I gotta go finish my homework," I say. I snatch his empty milk glass and quickly walk out of the room.

CHAPTER 19

THE KIDS AT school, they just won't let go of it—the story of the shooting.

In American history we're learning about the Revolutionary War. My cool, young history teacher, Mr. Nakleh, wants to start a discussion about the battle of Fort Ticonderoga. But before he can even flash the first image on the screen, A-Train's friend, Dunny Moore, yells out, "Here's an idea. Why don't we talk about what's happening right now?"

A-Train does the follow-up shout-out.

"Yeah, like why that pig Jeremy Hanson is walking the streets with a pistol by his side."

I can't make myself stay out of it. But my first punch barely lands.

"Hey, A. That Hanson cop is on desk leave, 'pending investigation,'" I say, and I immediately realize after a few groans and boos that I sound like the nerd-ball from hell.

"Pending investigation, pending investigation, pending-like-anyone-really-cares," says the girl who sits in front of me, the girl named TaTa, like in *good-bye*.

"You know the cop's going to get off."

The next kid to speak up is Louie Williams, the not-so-talented point guard on our basketball team.

To my amazement, Louie Williams actually gives a different point of view.

"You all, listen. This cop shot a gang member. You got that? This was a gang. They didn't show up to watch a Wizards game. They showed up to fight, to kill. Kick me if you wanna, but I'm voting with Ali on this."

A-Train gives a nasty laugh, then says, "Hey, Louie. Is your dad a cop, too?"

This whole little shouting match takes about twenty seconds, and I can't believe that Mr. Nakleh, who's young but can very easily be a hard-ass when he wants to, lets it go on this long.

No more waiting. Our teacher claps into action.

"Okay, if you're standing, sit down! If you're in this room, quiet down!" he shouts.

The class pretty much obeys, at least as much as we ever do.

"This whole Southeast thing is getting bigger and bigger, and I want to help focus on it, try to bring some sense to it, before it gets too big," Mr. Nakleh says.

A-Train shouts out again.

"Listen, man, if the police admitted that they..."

Mr. Nakleh outshouts him.

"I'm talking. So you are not talking. If you have a problem with that, leave the classroom right now."

A-Train does stop yelling. And Mr. Nakleh continues.

"Listen. The school is aware that there is a lot of

discussion, and disagreement, about the events last week with the gang bust and the police shooting. Yeah, everyone on both sides is very hot and angry. So it seems that maybe the time has come to have a more formal, and I might add, a more respectful conversation about what's happening. As you all know, Ms. Swanbeck is the moderator of the debate team. She suggests..."

This time TaTa interrupts.

"Let me guess. Ms. Swanbeck suggests a debate."

Mr. Nakleh snaps at TaTa, "You can move on out of the room, too, if you can't keep quiet."

"Sorry," says TaTa. Then quickly adds, "I'm just fed up with the cops."

Cedric pipes up. "And I'm fed up with the cops getting in trouble just for doing their jobs."

Mr. Nakleh gives a slight smile and says, "Well, well, well, I guess we have the two debaters to represent either side of the debate."

"Debate? In school? You mean talking and everything? Are you for real, Mr. N?" says Cedric. "There's no way I'm going to stand up in public and debate. I'm no public speaker."

Some kids in the class call him a few names (I won't write which ones) to make fun of him.

Mr. Nakleh looks around the room. "Do I have a volunteer replacement for Cedric?"

A-Train speaks immediately.

"Cedric can stop worrying. Because, listen, everyone knows who should represent the pro-cop side: the cop-loving cop kid himself."

A few voices shout my name.

"You cool with that, Ali?" Mr. Nakleh asks.

I say, "Sure," and the truth is, well, I am. I'd like to get this damn thing straightened out.

Mr. Nakleh continues. He is way over-enthused about this.

"Okay. So, it'll be Ali Cross representing, let's call it, 'The Police Dilemma.' TaTa, it's pretty clear you are the representative for the other side. Let's call that side 'The People's Dilemma.' "

TaTa pulls a Cedric.

"No way in this world," she says. "I'm not doing some formal debate. I will not be giving a speech. I'm a spontaneous talker. And for this talk, I'll be sitting in the back of the room with Cedric."

Pretty much everyone in the class laughs.

"Okay, okay," says Mr. Nakleh. "Everyone just calm down. We need a volunteer. Do we have a volunteer for the other side, the side representing the people?"

Mr. Nakleh says "the people" with extra emphasis. Why do I think that he might be a little more supportive of the anti-police side? Maybe I'm just fired up and, okay, maybe a little scared.

"So, a volunteer. We need a volunteer," says the man.

Then a voice, a nice voice, a strong voice, a voice I like, speaks up.

"Okay, I'll do it." Everyone turns to see who the volunteer is.

It's Sienna.

There's some applause. A few cheers.

"Going hard, girl!" yells TaTa. "I'll help you get ready."

"Okay," says Mr. Nakleh. "I'll tell Ms. Swanbeck about the debate, and she'll get in touch with Sienna and Ali, and now..."

He walks to the front of the classroom. He flips

open his laptop and says, "For now. Let's move on to Fort Ticonderoga. You may have heard of Ethan Allen and the Green Mountain Boys. Well, the British..."

For me, Mr. Nakleh's voice is fading, fading, fading. Then I'm not hearing it even one tiny little bit.

It's all sinking in. There's going to be a debate. A discussion. *With Sienna.*

Okay. Stay calm, Ali.

Okay. I'm good at thinking. I'm pretty good at talking. And, well, I've got to do this. After all, I'm the cop kid.

I look across a row of desks, and I see that Sienna is also looking across at me. I try to smile at her. But I don't think I get one back.

CHAPTER 20

I'M NOT SURE how the people who run Instagram let the fake @AliCross4Cops page stay up, even though I've reported it multiple times. But I'm kind of not surprised, given what I see when I scroll through people's pages. I gotta tell you: there's an awful lot of ugly stuff. To be honest, some of it is so dirty and mean that I can't (and I don't want to) give you examples. Sure, I'm pumped when I read posts from friends that support my point of view. But I'm just as super-mad when those people write nasty stuff about Sienna. Not that I plan on going easy on her myself when we debate.

Frankly, I'm worried. Word has started to spread about this debate, and social media seems to be supporting Sienna. I'm totally outnumbered.

YouTube has thousands of videos of cops using unnecessary force. And only a few videos of them helping a cat out of a tree.

But I've got numbers on my side. Major statistics about gang murders and assaults on innocent citizens. Plus my boys Cedric and Mateo have been filming interviews with people in our neighborhood—mostly people of color—talking about how the cops helped them.

From a tough-looking, tough-sounding teen:

"That officer on Benning Road where the shopping center is, he literally saved my mama's life. He stun-gunned the little punk who slashed my mama's wrist and arm and..."

From a middle-aged woman in a supermarket:

"There've been so many killings by the gangs, my husband says he slips and slides on all the bullet casings that litter the street."

Other people say things like, "We wouldn't be alive without the cops" and "They risk their lives every day. Who would even *want* a job like that?"

Hearing real people is going to be a powerful moment in the debate. But Sienna will have that, too, in the other direction. I have to remember that I still have to have the numbers, the charts, the facts. If not, Sienna will tear me apart.

I know I should resist checking Instagram again. But I can't. The posts are just as bad as before. Except now I'm getting some scary DMs, too. From people who think that fake Instagram account is me.

Enough of this. I've got a Spanish vocab quiz tomorrow that I've got to study for. But the minute I open my textbook, the front doorbell rings. I'm the only one at home. I look out the little side window to make sure it's not a protestor. I see a woman, maybe thirty years old, with black hair down to her waist. She's carrying a big leather satchel and wearing a blazer over nice jeans and a pair of blue-and-white Nikes.

"Good afternoon," she says as she flips open an ID case. It reminds me of the Washington, DC, police ID my dad carries. Only this woman's ID says "The Washington Post" right next to her photograph. (She looks a lot better in person.) But her name is too small to read. She soon fixes that.

"My name is Gloria Torres. I'm a reporter with the *Washington Post*."

"How do you do," I say politely.

"I'm fine, thanks. How are you?"

"Good. Thank you," I say, waiting for her to tell me why she's here.

"Are you by any chance Ali Cross?"

This does not feel right. And anyway, this kind of thing has happened a few times before. So I've been trained by Dad and Bree to be very cautious when a newspaper person comes around asking questions.

"I'm Ali Cross," I say, and then I quickly add, "I'd ask you in, ma'am, but I'm not allowed to talk to you."

"Why can't you talk to me? You believe in the First Amendment, right?" she asks. She's not pushy, but I don't think I'm letting her in. There's a pause.

I can tell immediately that she's the kind of person who has to fill silence. So because I didn't answer her question about the First Amendment as fast as she'd like, she decides to pitch it at me again.

"Ali, I repeat. You do believe in the First Amendment, don't you?"

As she asks the question again, she removes a small notepad from her leather bag. Then she clicks her pen and gets ready to write. A notepad? It's like something out of an old movie. Hasn't she heard about smartphones and recorders and iPads? But I move on to answer her question.

"Oh, yeah. I'm a total believer in the First Amendment," I say.

Then I can't stop myself from showing off.

"I can even tell you my favorite part of that amendment. 'Congress shall make no law abridging the freedom of speech, or of the press.' So, yes, I believe in the freedom to speak. And I also believe in the freedom *not* to speak."

"You know the amendment very well," she says. "Maybe I could step inside for a minute? We could talk about the First Amendment. Only the First Amendment."

I bite my lower lip (it's kind of a cute-guy pose

that sometimes works for me) and say, "No. I don't think so. I have a feeling that we'd end up talking about some other stuff."

"Like what?" she asks. She's acting all innocent, like I'm just being stubborn.

"Like all the craziness about the police and the shooting and the demonstrations."

"Well, what about them?" she says.

"No, ma'am. I'm not biting. I may be young, but I'm not that foolish. You and me are going to say good-bye."

"Ali Cross," she says. "You're young, but you are anything but foolish. In fact, I can tell that you are one impressive young man."

"Thanks," I say, but I'm still cautious. I don't think she's about to knock me over and run inside. But this conversation is over.

"Thank you, Ms. Torres. Stay safe."

"You, too, Ali," she says.

She turns around and steps down off the front stoop. The she stops and faces me again.

"Just one thing I want to let you know."

"Yeah?"

"I'm one determined, persistent, unstoppable reporter. So, like any good reporter, if there's a story here, I'll find a way to report it."

I bite my lower lip. Then I speak.

"Great. See you then."

Chapter 21

The Cross house on Tuesday night, 5:30 p.m. If you looked in on us, you would think that it was an ordinary American evening at home. But if you lived here, like me, you'd know this is a fairly special night, because this is one of the rare times that we are all together. Dad and Bree, who is also on the force, are not out on some police assignment. They're actually both home. That may not seem like a big deal for most families. But for us, it doesn't happen a whole lot.

The two of them are in the living room, probably

watching CNN. Nana Mama, of course, is doing something beneficial for mankind. She's at the dining room table tapping away at her laptop, filling out forms for her church's immigrant assistance program. Meanwhile, Jannie and I are scrounging around the fridge and the pantry closet, filling our faces with what we can find, which includes stale graham crackers, stale salt-free peanuts, and semisweet chocolate morsels, which I'm sure Nana was saving for baking chocolate chip cookies.

"I got an idea," I say.

"Go ahead," she says. I can tell Jannie's skeptical. She always is.

"How about you and I offer to make supper tonight?" I ask.

"Nana said that she was about to start making her chili-meatloaf. How about we stick with that? Everyone loves it," she says.

"Yeah, but maybe you and I could do something nice for the family."

Jannie is no fool. Now she turns suspicious.

"What exactly are you up to, Ali?" she asks. " 'Do something nice for the family'?"

"Okay. Forget it. I just thought it was a good idea."

"Good idea, huh? Here's my guess. One of the grown-ups is mad at you about something, and you want to suck up to them," Jannie says. But she must be into the idea, because she decides to go clear it with Nana.

Jannie is chuckling when she comes back into the kitchen. "Nana says we can do what we want. But I'm not sure she really means that. Because as I was walking out she said, 'Lord only knows what you and your brother are up to.' "

"Great," I say.

"So what'll we be cooking, chef?" Jannie asks.

I take a short survey of supplies. The only things in the fridge are ingredients for meatloaf: some chopped green peppers and a ton of uncooked hamburger meat. Okay, we'll be staying away from that.

I have not inherited the cooking gene from Nana Mama. So I can't juggle together the other ingredients I find in the kitchen—ketchup and American cheese and way too much broccoli—into something tasty. Then I do get an idea. And I share it with Jannie.

"There's some salad and bacon and a lot of eggs and four big fat potatoes in the vegetable bin. So I was thinking—breakfast for supper! Good idea, right?"

Jannie shrugs. I can tell she's not going to be much help. Enthusiastic? Not so much.

I try to get her excited. "Listen, it's cool. It's different. The whole deal—orange juice, toast. You know, breakfast for supper."

"They did that a lot in elementary school," Jannie says. "They used to have that 'breakfast for lunch.' I always thought it was kinda boring."

"I always thought it was kinda fun," I say. I get a shrug and a reluctant nod from my sister.

I tell her to start peeling the potatoes, and I'll start cracking the eggs into a bowl for the scramble. Actually, I've just checked out a very cool egg-cracking hack on my phone. You hold the egg in one hand, snap it against the rim of the bowl, and you hook your index finger inside of the shell and the egg should drop into the bowl. Like I said, that's what *should* happen. How does this hack work for me? Of course, it's a small disaster, egg yolk dripping all over the kitchen counter, egg white soaking my hand, bowl mostly empty.

Jannie gets the potatoes and takes a small paring knife from a drawer.

"You should use the potato peeler," I say.

"Nana always uses this little knife," she says.

"Yeah, but Nana is a pro," I say.

Then, in about two seconds, as if on cue, Jannie says, "Damn this knife." I look at her. A dot of blood has appeared on her left thumb. Her loud "Damn this knife" brings Nana into the kitchen immediately.

"What's with the cursing going on in here?"

(Nana should spend two minutes in the hallway of my middle school if she wants to hear what *real* cursing sounds like.)

"Why are you using that silly little knife, Jannie, when we've got an actual potato peeler?" Nana asks.

"Well, you always use..." Jannie begins.

Nana says, "Yeah, but I know what I'm doing." Then she adds, "You're lucky you escaped with such a teeny-tiny cut."

Okay, I was definitely worried when Jannie nicked herself, but after hearing Nana call her injury "teeny-tiny," I get the slight urge to tell her, *I told you so.*

"Let me wash my hands, and I'll peel those things for you," Nana says. A minute later she is peeling the potatoes so quickly that it looks like she's on fast-forward. But this is only the beginning of the circus that's coming into town.

Bree and Dad heard Jannie cry out from her cut, so they join us in the kitchen now. Bree immediately notices the scrap of paper towel wrapped around the tip of Jannie's thumb. The first thing my dad notices is the mess of egg guts sliding down the outside of my mixing bowl onto the counter.

"You don't crack an egg on the rim of the bowl," he says, and he decides to give me a demonstration. He lifts an egg from the carton and proceeds.

"You crack it on the countertop. That way the shell won't shatter and..."

But as he demonstrates his preferred egg-cracking method, he doesn't move fast enough between counter and bowl. Splat and spread!

"Nice, Dad," I say. "If the surface was hot enough, we could fry the egg right there."

My father laughs. He can't help it.

"Okay, camera's rolling. Take two," he says.

My dad creates the exact same mess again, and this time around Bree decides to comment.

"No, Alex. *In* the bowl. *In* the bowl." But she's laughing.

"I understand the concept, Bree," he says.

Direct from the potato-peeling department, Nana Mama says, "Are you sure you do?"

More laughter.

While the egg shenanigans are happening, I turn on the burner and unwrap the bacon. It looks like some new kind of bacon that Nana's bought. It's a stack of round slices—"rashers," Nana calls them. So I slice each one of the roundish pieces into strips, making them look the way bacon should look. Then I lay the slices out in Nana's amazingly heavy, amazingly hot cast-iron fry pan.

Within thirty seconds the rashers are turning brown, on their way to an ugly burnt black. Bree observes my bacon-cooking process.

"Whatever you're making, Ali, it's about to burn," she says. Oh, really? Good observation. That's what I'm thinking, but that's not what I say. I don't need to because Nana is immediately on top of it.

"You need some butter in that pan," Nana says as she finishes slicing the potatoes she's been peeling.

"There's smoke coming from it," Jannie says, and, helpful as always, she then pulls the faucet hose from the sink and douses the pan with water.

Steam and smoke start billowing. I guess it's sorta good: there is no doubt that the bacon is *not* burning anymore.

Nana turns around and looks at the drowning bacon.

"What on earth is boiling in that pan, Ali?" she asks.

"The bacon," I say. She looks in the pan.

"That's not bacon, young man. That there looks like somebody sliced up the bologna I bought for sandwiches."

Jannie and I both start cracking up, of course. I can tell that my dad wants to be stern about the whole situation, but Bree can't hold it in. She tries hard to keep her lips closed, but then she actually spits out a laugh. The craziness and laughter is contagious. Even my dad's big deep *hee-haw* fills the room.

Nana is the only one staying serious. Not because she doesn't appreciate the fun, but she's just too busy jumping around the cooking area. We watch her carry the ridiculously heavy pan over to the sink with oven mitts. She pours most of the boiling water from the pan right into the sink, losing just a few pieces of bologna along the way. Then she moves it back to the stovetop and drops in a big glob of butter. As the butter sizzles she adds her sliced potatoes and shakes the pan really hard. The potatoes start turning all brown and crispy. She gives them a good pinch of salt. Then she beats the eggs with a dinner fork and pours them in, too. She dumps in a bunch of spices from the spice rack, along with salt and pepper and a few big shots of Tabasco.

"I'm going to try and turn this disgusting mess into a real special omelet," she says. "You all go sit down."

But we're too hypnotized by Nana Mama's magic show to even move.

We watch as the "disgusting mess" starts to thicken. Then it starts to turn a pale yellow. Then it solidifies. Then it puffs up. Then Nana Mama lifts the pan.

"Quick, Bree! Get me a platter," Nana yells. Bree grabs an oversized plate.

Nana tips the pan and the omelet falls out perfectly, beautifully, onto the plate.

My dad, never much of a guy for joking around, yells out in a sort of phony preacher-type voice, "It's a miracle! It's a miracle!"

Of course, the rest of us laugh.

And as we should have expected, the omelet really is something of a miracle. It is incredibly delicious.

"Man, wow. This is sooo good," says Jannie.

"Yeah," I say. "We should do this every Tuesday."

CHAPTER 22

WE CARRY ON so much about Nana Mama's bologna omelet being delicious that as we eat it, we beg her like little kids to take the leftover eggs and make another. Dad doesn't join in on the begging. He's really into being "the grown-up in the room."

Then Jannie points out that we have no more bologna. No prob. Nana Mama says that she had a few uncooked hot dogs hidden in the back of the fridge and that "frankfurters are nothing but bologna meat all pushed into a sausage casing." So

Dad and I share another (but smaller) omelet. Then we have a contest as to which of us can moan the loudest because we're so full.

Okay, Jannie was right. My real reason for coming up with the whole "breakfast-for-supper" idea was to get back on Nana's (who knew I was sneaking around) and Dad's (who also knew I was sneaking around, even if he didn't want to talk about it) good sides. It all worked out for me on so many levels. Peace. Calm.

I'm lying in bed right now and I'm barely thinking about the debate and Ms. Swanbeck and Sienna and the whole class watching us. I'm not even thinking about the fact that I've still got a week of bullying and name-calling and even a possible physical fight before the actual debate itself. Full of bologna and hot dogs and eggs, I'm doing some school reading and I'm ready to turn out the light when...damn it all...I hear my phone *ping* with a new alert message from Gabe's police scanner app.

I read my screen and find out that a "disturbed/disoriented woman, age approx. eighty-five, is causing disruption in Q Street and Minnesota area." The report is followed by a text from Gabe. Of course, Gabe had not recently eaten a ten-pound omelet. So he's at peak enthusiasm about this police alert.

Here's his text.

C U on Q and Min near monument in 10 mins.

Damn again. Now I've got moral dilemmas and ethical dilemmas popping up all over the place. I won back Nana's trust and possibly even my father's trust, and here I am thinking of sneaking out for another police adventure.

I make that funny face—the one where you squint your eyes real tight—like that's going to help you decide. But this time it doesn't help me. My eyes just hurt. I make a decision. Unfortunately, all that squinting helps me to make the wrong decision, of course. As I get ready, I'm even sort of hoping that Nana or Bree or my dad will hear me, and I'll be forced to abandon the mission. But no such bad luck. Gabe is waiting, and I've got to move.

I sneak out of my house as smooth as a cat burglar, and ten minutes later I'm huddled behind a dumpster with Gabe. But no other onlookers are on the 1900 block in the Fairlawn neighborhood. No cops, either.

A few words here about Fairlawn. It's part of Southeast, and, in my opinion, it is the nicest part. There are some pretty big houses here, sweet front porches, swing sets and seesaws and new cars in the driveways.

"I don't see anything, Gabe. It's a ghost town—a very clean, quiet ghost town," I say. "No cops. No cruisers. No nothing."

"You're right, man," he says. "Wait... do you hear that? I think it's coming from over there. Come on."

I follow Gabe as we creep down the block. Across the street, I see an old bent-over woman screaming at a man standing in the open front door. The porch light comes on, and I see the scene clearly now. The man is in his underwear. It's not a pretty sight. He's in torn boxers and a Superman T-shirt. The bent-over lady, well, she's just wearing a whole closetful of clothes in all kinds of colors and states: old, torn, dirty. Both the man and the woman are agitated.

"Let me in or I'll burn your house down and you'll burn in Satan's fire with all the other demons," the woman screams.

"What is wrong with you, old woman? Why are you going around ringing doorbells at one in the morning? You're nothing but a crack-headed old hag!"

Then the man shoves her. She stumbles backward. I understand his frustration, but he's being really rough with her. Problem is, I don't think he's going to calm down.

"Get the hell out of here," he yells.

Now we see the front porch light go on at the house next door. A young couple—she's in a bathrobe, he's in pajama bottoms—yells across to their neighbor. "She was just banging on our doors, front and back, screaming like a fool!"

"You know who that is, Ali, right?" says Gabe.

"Course I do. It's just Screaming Sally. She's not going to hurt anyone."

"Probably not, but who would want Screaming Sal knocking on their door this late at night?"

Although I'm surprised to see her in the fancier

Fairlawn section, I can't remember a time that Screaming Sally wasn't a part of the neighborhood. She was never exactly dressed in rags, but the clothes she wore were old-looking: a big, heavy red skirt that brushed against the dirty street, some sort of bright yellow-and-purple blanket she used as a shawl. In wintertime she sometimes walked around in three overcoats at once.

If Nana Mama and I saw her on the street, Nana would talk to her a little, and as we walked away, she'd tell me, "The woman's had a rough time of it. You be sure to be kind to her."

Sometimes I did try to talk to Sally. Usually she was pretty nice. Hell, she was very nice. She'd ask you about school. She'd ask if you were being good to your parents. But then, every once in a while, she'd just explode with...you got it...uncontrollable screaming and howling. Like once, on N Street, she came running up to me and began yelling right in my face.

I saw what you did! I saw you steal that car! I saw you touch that girl! You can't fool me. You will burn for all eternity. You will turn to ashes like an old cigar butt!

I was terrified, but usually she'd scream and then run away. But I guess this was not one of those nights. Tonight she seems to be on some kind of a bender.

A police car pulls up in front of the house. I think about taking out my cell phone to start filming what happens next. But it doesn't feel right to record Sally when she's acting like this.

The old gal makes her way down the front steps and then crosses the front lawn and walks up the steps of the next house over. The young couple there are sort of standing guard behind their glass door. That's not going to stop Sally. She walks right up to their door and starts yelling in their faces.

"You gotta let me in. You gotta. The cops are here! And they hate me. They'll shoot me. They will. They want to shoot me. If you don't let me in, they'll kill me."

By now the police officers have gotten out of their car and are approaching Sally and the young couple. I'm kind of worried, especially when Sally starts throwing wasted punches at the two cops, one a young white female officer, the other an older Black guy. But neither one of them touches Sally.

"Leave me alone, you bastards! Kill me. Go ahead. Kill me. Try to kill me. You think the president doesn't care about me. He does. He does. Don't mess with me. I know the president. Him and me are friends."

"We're not going to mess with you, Sal. We just need you to calm down a little bit," says the woman cop. And now she does touch Sally, but only to put her own arm gently up and around Sally's shoulder.

"Aren't you living over at the Monroe Shelter?" says the other officer.

"No. They threw me out. The scum threw me out," Sally says. She's angry. But she's becoming quieter. She speaks softly. "I was having trouble sleeping. So I started to sing. And then they threw me out."

All of a sudden, Sally starts crying.

The woman officer speaks.

"I don't think they really threw you out, Sally. In fact, they were scared when they saw you were missing. That's why they called us. They want you back. They told us."

I'm surprised at that. I was expecting more of a fight.

Maybe I wouldn't even have blamed the officers if they'd needed to restrain her. Sally was acting scary, like she'd really hurt someone. But they're treating Sally like... like... like she's a human being.

Two more officers and a fire ambulance now show up, but the two working officers who have been there from the beginning shake their heads and wave the new guys off.

"It's all under control," the female officer says. The few other neighbors who have come out to watch the commotion head back inside their houses. The red light on the ambulance twirls and twirls, adding way too much drama to what ended up being a very undramatic situation.

Sally stands perfectly still. She looks confused, like she doesn't know where she is.

The officers help Sally into the back of their police car. The male officer says, "Okay, we're ready. We're going to get you back safe and sound and into bed."

They let her take her time getting into the car. The female officer slides in next to old Sally.

The other officer quickly spins around and looks

directly at me and Gabe, who had come closer to watch the scene.

"And you two guys. The same advice. Go back home and get to bed. And if you don't want to walk back home, we'll give you a ride. I'm sure your parents will be glad to see you getting out of a police car."

Screaming Sally gives Gabe and me a wide smile and a big wave through the car's rear window.

As we start the short walk back to our homes, Gabe says, "I definitely thought that was going to end differently. But they were so nice with her. Helping her, getting her calm. Taking her back to the shelter."

"Yeah, the cops were really great," I say. "No wonder so many people hate them."

CHAPTER 23

NANA MAMA GOES to church every Sunday. And we go with her, whether we like it or not.

"Jesus is expecting you," she always says. And then she adds, "And we certainly are not going to disappoint Him."

It's always the eleven o'clock Mass up at St. Anthony's where Jesus is expecting the Cross family.

If my dad is home—the only reason he can ever miss Mass is if he's working an emergency—then he and Bree join us. When Mass ends (and it takes a while, what with all the choir songs and preaching and praying and the priest asking for donations) my dad goes over to the church hall and helps out at the soup kitchen. Sometimes he takes me with him, and when he does that he always tells me the same thing: "If someone asks you to do something, just go ahead and do it. It's always best to be helpful." Being helpful for me seems to entail the endless unfolding of folding chairs, the occasional mopping of the kitchen floor, and, worst of all, the endless rinsing out and scrubbing of all the pots and pans and cups and plates. Then, of course, there's always this annoying little thing. People ask me one certain question over and over again: "You're the detective's boy, aren't you?"

Everything at church is the same from week to week. Nana dresses up, sometimes even wearing a hat. We all walk through the center entrance doors and into the church. Nana always insists on walking down the center aisle to get a "good seat up front." Dad says she'd sit on the altar if they let her.

I hate that walk down the aisle. I know that we're

all being looked at—not necessarily in a rude way, but still, people are watching us.

Nana marches straight ahead like a fast-walking happy bride who can't wait to get married. Dad and Bree walk a bit slower, and Dad smiles at all the people he knows (and that's a lot of people). Sometimes he'll even stop to shake somebody's hand or give some lady a quick kiss on the cheek.

More than once I've heard Nana tell him that he walks through the church "like a man who's running for mayor."

His answer is always the same: "Well, maybe someday I will run for mayor. So this is good practice."

Jannie hates the walk as much as I do, but for different reasons. She is sure that everyone is studying her, judging her. She'll say later on, "I think everybody hated my salmon-colored hoodie." I'll say, "How could you even know that?" She'll say, "Because I just know. Don't you understand?" I guess I don't.

But today, with all the publicity, I know how she feels. It's not just that I see heads turning as we make our formal entrance, it's that I can hear people.

"That's the Cross boy."

"Look. The father is with them. I know him pretty well. Good man. Good man."

"That's the father. I've met him. A little too sure of himself if you ask me."

"That's the boy who's arguing for the cop's side in that school debate."

On and on. I try to ignore it. Fat chance.

The story sells itself. Dramatic. Dangerous. Local. So everybody in Southeast has strong opinions about the shooting, and the folks in Southeast are not shy about making their opinions heard. Yes, there have been two district council meetings about "The Future of Proper Policing." Yes, a formal investigation into Officer Hanson's conduct has been set up. And, unfortunately (in my opinion), news about our middle school debate has really captured the imagination of a lot of people in this part of DC.

It's become well-known enough that the debate has even been opened to the public. ("It's a *public* school, okay?" Mateo reminded me a little harshly.) In fact, the whole ridiculous thing has been moved to the auditorium. Okay, it's not the main stage at the Kennedy Center, but for Ali Cross it is totally frightening.

Anyway, because of all this focus on the debate, I'm hating my life quite a lot as we walk down the main aisle this particular Sunday.

I try to see—without looking too obvious—if Sienna is in the congregation. Jannie sees me twisting my head around slightly, and, of course, she's immediately on to me. So she nudges me hard as we're walking and says, "Quit looking for your little crush. She and her folks go to the First Baptist Church."

I didn't know that, and actually that's good news.

I do see A-Train, though. He's sitting with his parents. The three of them are looking pretty stern. They see me (you can't miss the Cross parade), and they look straight at me, and then turn away fast. I mean, come on. Be nice. This is church.

As we walk the endless walk, I sometime catch a nod or a smile or a wave from one or two people.

But not many. Oh, man, it feels like it's taking a few hours to get to the end of this aisle.

Finally, we make it to our seats and the Mass begins.

The organ music swells, and a serious-looking bunch of men and women walk on to the altar with the priest. Then everybody stands and starts singing a hymn. It's always the same one: "The Lord Will Bring Me Peace." I join in because, boy, do I hope that happens.

A shuffling of papers, a shuffling of feet. Everyone stands. "In the name of the Father, and of the Son..." Father Hannigan begins. Then another hymn. Then some guy on the altar reads an epistle. Then...I really can't tell you a lot more. I am on another planet. And I stay on that planet through the rest of the service.

All I want to do is get home.

Outside, at the bottom of the church steps, a small group of people gathers around us. People always like a meet-and-greet with Dad and Bree and Nana. But this feels a little different. I suddenly realize that most of the ten or twelve folks gathered around us are looking at me.

One of the men, someone I don't even recognize, grabs my shoulder.

"Good luck with everything, Ali," he says.

My bio lab partner's mom says, "We're with you, Ali."

"I'll be watching and rooting for you."

"You'll be great."

And this is the part where I should tell you that because of these people and their kindness and good wishes, all my doubts and fears just disappear. I should tell you that I was ready for the debate. I'd show them all. I was a winner.

Yeah, I could lie and tell you all that. But I can't. Because as you know, I just came from church.

CHAPTER 24

"SO, YOU'LL BE helping out at the soup kitchen, right, son?"

There is a two-word answer to that question. The first word is "yes," and the second is "Dad." Sweet and simple.

Ten minutes later I'm up to my elbows in hot greasy water, scraping the burnt-on food from giant metal pots. I'm way too tough to use rubber gloves like a reasonably intelligent person. So my fingers keep burning, and the greasy pots keep slipping out of my hands. And if you were wondering whatever happened to Jannie after the Mass, and why she isn't up to her elbows in water, well, the reason is that she has a Sunday morning job as a dog walker. And that sounds a lot better than washing dishes in a soup kitchen.

Speaking of the soup kitchen, I'll tell you about it. St. Anthony's soup kitchen is like a giant indoor block party. And it should probably be called a meal kitchen, since I've never seen them actually serve soup. An amazing number of people come to the Sunday meal, at least four hundred. On really cold Sundays, a lot of people come to the place just to get warm. Most of the people are from the neighborhood. Some folks bring their kids and their cousins and their aunts and their uncles. You can always count on there being a lot of old people joining the meal. Bree says that the elderly are "the overlooked poor in America."

I'm stacking some pots on the super-big drying rack when I hear a voice. It's a big voice, a gentle voice, a voice I know really well.

"Hey, I think you missed a spot of macaroni there, young man. Better start all over."

It's my dad's best friend, John Sampson. He keeps talking.

"Before the Mass I told Father Hannigan to have you come up to the pulpit and give the sermon. That way you could get some practice talking in front of a crowd," Detective Sampson says.

For a split second, I panic. In the next split second, he cracks up laughing. Yes, I can be kind of gullible sometimes.

Then Detective Sampson says, "You'd better get back to work, Ali. It'd be pretty embarrassing to get fired from a volunteer job. Plus, it would be even more embarrassing for it to happen before your big debate."

Your big debate. *My* big debate. *The* big debate.

Sampson punches me (a little too hard) on my arm and then goes off to help bring out more food from the warming oven. Me? I look around and see people looking for second helpings, while most of the cooks and servers are mopping their foreheads in the overheated room.

I suddenly remember one of Nana Mama's favorite expressions: "You can always find a way to make yourself useful." Then she always adds, "If you can't, then you're not trying hard enough."

So I try. And I guess I do try hard enough because I spend the next fifteen minutes helping one older lady cut her pork cutlet into really tiny little pieces. Then I help another lady trade in her scrambled eggs and ham steak for two donuts. I bus about a hundred dirty dishes, refill about a hundred coffee cups, and after I help myself to a bowl of Ms. Leone's Chinese chili, I notice that there's another sink full of dirty plates that need some serious scrubbing.

I consider avoiding this job. But then I hear some guy's voice behind me.

"Those plates over there have your name on them, son."

I think I'll wear the rubber gloves this time out.

CHAPTER 25

THE JOBS THEY assign me at the soup kitchen almost always suck, but I've got to say, when my two hours are over, I usually feel pretty good. Basically, I like helping fine people eat some good food and have a good time.

But next day when I'm back at school, things are still pretty bad. Okay, there's my own little group of friends, who are always there for me no matter what. That helps. What doesn't help is that they keep asking questions like, "What are you gonna say?" or "Aren't you nervous?" or "Do you think this is gonna ruin your chances with Sienna?" I tell them that I don't need them to drive me up the wall, that I can do it entirely by myself. But they keep trying.

From where I stand, the opposition feels a lot stronger. They've got the passion. They make the noise. They rally around one simple belief: that cops use too much force. They don't see police work as some sort of delicate balance between doing the right thing and the tough thing. They see it as bad people doing a bad job.

Here would be a typical argument between me and them:

"That porker didn't have to cuff Mikey," says someone.

"But Mikey had just cut the newsstand guy," I say.

"It was nothing—a stupid little cut," says the kid.

"But it was a cut, a robbery, an attack!" I say.

"It was nothing."

"It was something."

So, without my noticing, my opponent hijacks the argument. It's not that he's smarter than me, he's just more determined than me. The debate right here this time is no longer about assault or slashing. It's about whether the officer should have done more than slap some cuffs on a kid who could have killed someone. Yeah, debate depends on brains. But it seems that it also depends on cunning and strategy. I'm not sure I'm any good at either of those.

"But he was hurting someone. He was committing a crime," I say.

"Maybe so. Who cares? They didn't have to treat him so badly. The cops are out of control."

"They weren't out of control this time. They were stopping a kid from hurting someone."

So that's school. That's how it goes.

Then there's Sienna. When I run into her, she and I talk, but the words come slowly, and we both sound pathetic and shy. It's a lot of "How you doing?" and "Doing okay. How about you?" and then "You ready for Thursday?" and "Trying to be ready." Then, nervous laughter.

"See ya."

"Yeah, okay."

"Luck, Sienna."

"Luck, Ali."

Every minute of every day makes me a little more nervous. And I've got the stories to prove it.

Next example. Every word is true.

The bathroom is a place I now try to avoid. Until it's unavoidable. Yeah, they have security guards walking in and out, but there are two problems with the security guards at our school. The first one is that they can no longer tell the difference between the smell of weed and the normal bathroom smells, and secondly, all they do is take a quick look around the room, jot down some sort of check-in on their devices, and then they disappear. So you're usually on your own, even when your bladder's about to explode.

Okay, you don't have to be a Marine recon trainee to know that if you want to avoid trouble in the boys' room, do *not* use a urinal. A stall seems a little safer. Step in, slide the lock closed behind you, do what you have to do, and get out. Hope that some bully doesn't try to crawl beneath the stall door to try to pull you off the toilet (think I'm making this up? It happened twice to Mateo).

Anyway, today I opt for the stall, even though I really don't need it. Then I do what I need to. I zip up. When I step out of the stall, though, I've got a surprise. The boys' room is usually pretty crowded, but today, as soon as I unlatch the door to the stall, I see that it's unusually empty. In fact, there's just one other guy in there. This other guy doesn't look at all familiar, but he does look large, mighty large, six-feet large, maybe. He's standing at one of the sinks, and he's doing a really bad job of pretending to wash his hands. I give my own nervous fingers a quick rinse, and then I head for the door. I will definitely air-dry my hands.

As I open the main exit door to leave the bathroom the six-feet-tall guy in the bathroom yells loudly, "Cop kid! Cop kid! Cop kid on the loose!"

CHAPTER 26

I'M OUT IN the hallway now with four other kids—the guy who was in the bathroom, two girls, and another guy. I think that I know almost everyone in my school. Even if I haven't talked to them, I can at least identify them. But I swear I've never seen any of these kids before, and I also swear that they are all bigger than me, taller than me, older than me, even the girls (who are not really girls but women). The worst thing is that these kids look way meaner and tougher than me.

The two girls are each kneeling down on one knee, the two guys standing with their feet wide apart. They are all facing me. But here's the freaky part: They are all pointing their hands at me, their index fingers aimed like the barrel of a pistol. All four "shooters" make that dumbass bullet-firing sound.

Puh-kuh. Puh-kuh. Loud. Very loud. *Puh-kuh.*

They fake shoot. Then they fake shoot some more. Occasionally one of them will bend his arm up, then snap it down and resume shooting. They seem to think that this is particularly clever. They laugh as they pull this move.

They are so totally enjoying themselves. And I hate myself for actually being scared. It's absurd. Stupid big kids acting like stupid little kids playing cops and robbers.

Then I suddenly hear a very loud voice.

"What the hell are you guys doing?"

I turn my head to see who's yelling.

It could be one of the assistant principals. Or a teacher. Or Coach Hassim.

But it turns out to be way better than any of

those people. It turns out that it's my good friend Cedric. All 175 pounds of my good friend Cedric. His face is turned way up to very mean and very angry. He's wearing his XXL Army surplus jacket, and his left hand is patting some bulging, bulky item in that jacket.

Looks like the question—*What are you doing?*—is going to go unanswered as a few nervous seconds go by.

"Just having fun with the cop kid," one of the girls finally says. She acts like this is no big deal. She pretends that she doesn't care that someone caught them, but the other three—they're nervous. Suddenly, they don't look like they're having as much fun. They even put down their "weapons," sort of.

"You know what? It doesn't look to me like the cop kid is having fun," says Cedric.

By now, the hallway is busy and a few kids start to crowd around. But I know they don't want to get too involved, in case this little scene grabs a teacher's attention. I know if I was passing by this spectacle, I would definitely move on. But I can't really do that now, can I? So I'm not too surprised when I see everyone glance at us and then keep walking. The only face in the crowd I actually recognize is Gabe's, and he stands on the edge of the action.

"Hey, man, we were joking, you know, joking around," says the guy who was in the boys' room with me. He's trying to stay tough, but I get the sense, deep down, that his "chicken" is showing. Cedric keeps patting his side pocket.

"Yeah, well. Why don't you just leave Ali alone," says Cedric. I watch—we all watch—as Cede now slips his hand into his pocket.

Cedric speaks again.

"Who the hell are you guys, anyway?"

There's no answer.

We're all waiting (and I'm privately saying a thank-you prayer for Cedric), but before anything else happens the school emergency siren goes off—piercing, ugly. The loudspeaker comes on:

"PLEASE RETURN TO THE NEAREST CLASSROOM OR FACULTY ROOM. STUDENTS ARE NOT ALLOWED TO REMAIN IN THE HALLWAYS OR

STAIRWELLS. PLEASE RETURN TO THE NEAREST CLASSROOM. TEACHERS AND SECURITY WILL PATROL ALL HALLS AND STAIRWELLS."

The four strangers take off. Fast. I watch them all reach the closest fire exit door. A very loud fire alarm begins to beep. And as the gang of four run through the door, one of the guys turns and shoots the last couple of imaginary bullets at me. Now, in addition to the beeping fire alarm, the loudspeaker repeats:

"PLEASE RETURN TO THE NEAREST CLASSROOM...."

Then it's all over. No more siren. No more fire alarm. No more announcements.

"Who the hell were those jokers?" Gabe asks.

"Fools. Just fools," Cedric says.

"I hope that's *all* they were," says Gabe.

Okay, the noise has stopped. Two security guards and a few teachers come into the hall.

A new loudspeaker announcement informs us that "THE EMERGENCY HAS ENDED. PLEASE RETURN TO YOUR CLASSROOMS IMMEDIATELY."

"I bet those four aren't even from our school,"

says Gabe. "No wonder they ran out through the side entrance."

We all should be taking off to our classrooms. But first, there's something I've got to ask Cedric.

"What were you thumping on inside your pocket, Cede?"

"Two very dangerous objects." He smirks at me. "A smartphone and a Nature Valley bar."

We would usually be laughing at something like this. We don't. But I do speak.

"Thanks for what you did, C," I say.

"Hey, anytime the threat is completely fake, you can count on me."

"No, man," I say. "I really mean it. You didn't have to do that."

"Yeah, of course I did," Cedric says. "You're my boy."

CHAPTER 27

MY HOUSE IS practically empty.

Jannie is over at Howard University pounding the track, like she does every Monday, completely determined to break a four-minute mile.

Bree and my dad are out doing their jobs. The house is only occupied by me and Nana Mama. And she's downstairs fixing supper (I can smell the onions cooking) and singing (Nana's old CD player is blasting out her favorite gospel singer, CeCe Winans, who is belting "Never Lost").

You've never lost a battle
And I know you never will

Whatever you say, CeCe.

As for me right now? I'm trying to decide whether to start my homework or study up on my debate material. Instead, still trying to calm myself down after what happened at school, I decide to sharpen my video game skills.

I'm just about to jump into my season with the Wizards on NBA 2K22 when my police app chimes. Daytime. Unusual. Most serious calls—shootings, drugs, gangs—are nighttime problems. Not sunny, four p.m. problems.

I read it. This'll make you nervous. A missing child.

Four-year-old girl. White T-shirt, turquoise shorts, purple KUBUA sneakers. She answers to the name Yolanda Curtis. Last seen PSP/AP.

I don't need the local Southeast police department manual to tell me what those initials stand for: Pirate Ship Playground at Anacostia Park, a pretty nice spot that kids really love. Fun, clean, entertaining. And way too near the Anacostia River for a playground.

My first problem, of course, is how to get out of my house without setting off alarms with Nana Mama. Sneaking away is out of the question in broad daylight. And, as the past has proven, lying to Nana is not a smart alternative.

I toy with the idea of telling her the truth. Hmmm. Let me just think about that.

Okay, that takes me about a second. *No.*

I text Gabe and Cedric. They tell me they're on their way to the Pirate Ship Playground. I let them know that there might be a slight delay. I call it the "Nana-Mama" delay.

I walk down the stairs. I enter the kitchen. I'm calling up all my bad acting skills so I can look calm and casual. Meanwhile, that app on my phone won't quit dinging and vibrating every few seconds.

"Hey, Nana. You're steppin' hard to your CeCe Winans tunes. Nice," I say. "Very nice."

"Best thing that ever happened at St. Anthony's church was when the monsignor agreed to let Martin and Bettina and me bring that gospel group in to sing after communion," she says. "I love that it's a regular Sunday thing."

"Everybody's lovin' it," I say. (And the truth is, everybody does love it.)

Nana suddenly looks very serious. I could swear that her eyes squint a little bit as she stares straight at me. She's looking at me hard. Or I should say that she's looking *through* me hard.

"You know, Ali. I believe that I've got a special sixth sense about you," she says.

"Oh, you really think so?" I say. I could swear my voice is actually shaking.

Meanwhile, my own sixth sense tells me: this is not going to go well.

"Let me give you an example of what I mean," Nana says.

She stands up extra-straight and speaks. She's talking like she's a fortune-teller or something, but she's not being silly.

"Ali, I sense that you are about to tell me that you want to go out. And when I ask if you've finished your homework, I sense that you'll say 'My homework is almost completely finished.' Then I'll ask, 'You all set for the big debate?' and you'll say, 'Of course I am, Nana.' Then I'll ask who all you are going to be seeing, and you'll say Cedric or Gabe or Mateo. How'm I doin' so far?"

"I'd say good, pretty good." And Nana keeps going.

"Then I'll say, 'Is it a safe place you're going to?' and you'll say, 'Of course, Nana. Perfectly safe.' And so I'll say, 'Well then, go on out, Ali,' because I know there's no use trying to force you to stay put."

Neither of us speaks for a few seconds. I'm scared to move, like Nana Mama didn't really just give me permission to go out.

Then she asks, "Did I leave something out?"

"Yes. The most important part. What do you always say when I'm walking out the door?"

I go to the kitchen door and open it before she can change her mind.

"'Don't forget to come home,'" I say. And then I'm gone.

CHAPTER 28

BAD THINGS SEEM a lot worse when they happen on a bright sunny day. That's how it is for all the officers and firefighters and volunteers who are walking and looking and praying for Yolanda Curtis. Yo-Yo to her friends and family.

You can hear babies crying, some toddlers yelling, the usual neighborhood sirens wailing, but mostly you hear grown-up voices shouting some version of Yolanda Curtis's name.

"Yolanda. Yolanda."

"Lonnie. Lonnie."

"Yo-Yo. Yo-Yo. Yo-Yo."

Cedric and Gabe are there. I walk over to meet them, but before I can say anything, we overhear a police officer breaking down the case to another one. We sneak closer to listen in. The officer is explaining what happened.

"The missing child was being watched by her big sister. The big sister, well, she isn't more than ten or eleven years old herself."

That happens a lot around here. Kids taking care of other kids. Or even worse, little kids being left alone.

The police officer shrugs as he talks.

"Their mom isn't around much, and her kids live in the Millicent Public Projects two streets up. You know the place. Everyone 'round here calls it the Millie House."

Yeah, the officer is right. Everyone knows the Millie House. It's a place to buy drugs. It's a place to stay away from.

The officer keeps talking.

"Anyway. It's not official or anything, but I think

the older sister might have been using or something, and, you figure, the little girl is only four. The big sister is eleven. The sisters' ages between them barely adds up to sixteen. It's a shame.

"So the little one. Yolanda. Sometimes they call her Yo-Yo. She goes out from the ground-floor apartment, and since they live so close, she actually knows how to get herself over to the park. They go there a lot, her and her sister. This is not good. I don't hold out much hope for finding the kid."

"You don't? Really?" the other officer asks.

"Nah. I don't. The little girl was missing for over an hour before we got a call-in about her."

"Shit," says Cedric. I see he's shaking a little. He closes his lips tight, and his cheeks balloon out a little, too. I keep myself steady, but this whole thing is making us sick. I can see I'm not the only one who's scared.

Cede is the biggest guy of the three of us. He's absolutely the strongest. All things considered, he's got to be the bravest. You know. Brave, like sure of himself.

An older officer gestures for the other officers to

join him. The first officer nods that he's coming, and says to the other, "Over there. That's the sister. I'm gonna go see what they found out from her."

He takes one step in the direction of the big sister. Then he notices me.

"You're Alex Cross's son, aren't you?" he asks.

"Yessir," I say.

"Good luck on that debate you got coming up," he says. "It means a lot to us folks on the force."

Cedric, Gabe, and I watch the officers walk over toward a very skinny girl in short shorts and a Georgetown T-shirt.

I stare into the Anacostia River. It's one ugly sight. Especially this part of the river here. The water is brown where I'm standing, and it's filled with all sorts of nasty stuff—tires and old bikes and plastic trash bags, even a car. If you stand near the crumbly shore, you can see the world's largest collection of empty bottles of no-name cognac and Dr Pepper.

Cedric bows his head and closes his eyes. I know how he feels. It's that nauseating feeling you get when you're afraid. I look out at the river. I keep thinking of what Nana Mama has told me and

Jannie more than a few times: "It takes only two inches of water for a person to drown."

The stink from the Anacostia is getting to us. So I'm not surprised when Cedric suddenly throws up. I'm just surprised when I manage not to do the same thing.

Then Gabe speaks, and he sounds impatient, almost angry.

"Get it together, dudes. We've got to help look for that kid."

CHAPTER 29

SO WE LOOK. We look hard. We have a strategy. Wherever we do *not* see cops or other searchers, then that's where we go looking.

We crawl under an unbelievably big willow tree at the river's edge. The tree has hundreds, maybe thousands, of droopy branches that practically touch the ground. The area under the tree is muddy and smells awful. Enough garbage and chicken bones and old cigarette butts to get us nauseous all over again. No Yo-Yo. No little girl.

"Look in here," Gabe shouts. It's a very big square hole in the ground that's covered by a rotted wooden doorway. The lock on the doorway is broken, and we shoot rock paper scissors to decide who should climb down inside and take a look.

I lose.

Once I'm inside, the muddy floor squishes and oozes beneath me. There is still enough afternoon light from above that I can make out a few dirty catcher's masks, a lot of beer cans, and—what the hell?—two books: a really nice leather-bound Holy Bible in good condition and a soggy falling-apart copy of *The Call of the Wild,* which my dad had been telling me forever to read. This sort of freaks me out. The Bible and the other book are surprisingly clean. Someone has been here recently. But there's no sign of a kid.

I climb back out, and we check some areas where other searchers have probably already looked. Because, hey, you never know.

"Maybe we'll catch something the adults missed," says Gabe.

"Yeah? Like what?" I ask.

"Man, I don't know...a shoe or something."

That doesn't make any sense to me, but what do I know?

"You know. A shoe. Like a clue. A shoe or a glove or a necklace," says Gabe.

"Yeah," I say. "We get it. We know what a clue is."

We all keep looking.

I replay the officer's words: *I don't hold out much hope. I don't hold out much hope. I don't...*

"Over here, clowns," Gabe says. He's standing on a small hill. The hill is not much bigger than a pitcher's mound. Cedric and I rush on over.

"Look at this," Gabe says.

Embedded in the grassy little mound is a handle pull. As Cedric lifts the handle, a dirt-covered door opens. We look into it. It's some sort of storage hole.

I know. I know.

You're expecting me to tell you now that something wonderful happens, like we hear a child sobbing or snoring or crying. But we don't. We don't hear a thing.

This underground area, no bigger than a closet,

is filled with the same kind of junk that we saw in the other storage area. And, get ready for this, there are two moldy copies of *The Call of the Wild* resting right here, on a pile of crumpled beer cans. I guess some school nearby assigned that book.

Searchers keep searching, but the day is starting to turn a little darker. The sun is a tiny bit weaker. I guess there are a lot of police officers and volunteers walking and looking. But the fact is, a four-year-old, Yo-Yo, with her little legs, could only get herself so far. And I know that Gabe and Cedric and I won't say out loud what we are all thinking. Did she fall into the river? Did someone scoop her up and take her away?

Keep looking. Keep looking. Some of the other people who were standing by, hoping and praying and watching, start to leave. Time for supper. Time for me to get home, too. But I can't give up. If I'm late, I'll deal with Nana. It won't be the first time and it won't be the last time. I think she'll understand.

Keep looking.

I stand at the river's edge. What if I saw a little body? What if I looked down and...

I do see something.

A grown-up, leaning against a bridge that goes over the river. They're very short and very thin. Their face is so covered with dirt and grime that I am not sure if they're Black or white, young or old, or even a man or a woman.

Unhoused, obviously. Mentally ill, maybe, but I'm not sure. It's getting harder and harder to tell anymore.

But I can tell that something just doesn't feel right.

I stare, trying to figure it out. They're wearing a filthy, torn pink polo shirt, the kind with the little green alligator on it, and they're holding a huge, very dirty, stained cotton sack in their hands. The sack looks heavy.

I'm nervous, but something inside me makes me walk up to them.

"Uh, excuse me? Have you seen a little girl around here lately?" I ask.

"Why? Didja know her?" they say. They clutch the cotton sack a little tighter.

I tremble just a little. I'm suddenly cold. I think I'm going to cry. Or throw up.

Because I'm pretty sure I know what—*who*—is in that sack.

"There's a church soup kitchen not too far from here," I say. "If you let me look inside that bag, I can take you there. Help you get some food. I bet you're hungry."

The person grunts, like they're considering it. They start to let go of the sack.

I make my move. I pull the bag out of their hands and tear it open.

Two big round eyes blink up at me.

The little girl. It's her. Yo-Yo.

"She's in here!" I yell. "Help!"

The girl doesn't speak. She doesn't cry. She's so little, smaller than I thought a four-year-old could be, and she still has her tiny little shoes on. She has brown stuff—chocolate?—around her mouth.

Gabe and Cedric come running over to me, and begin yelling the magic words.

"We found her. We found her. We've got her!"

The person who had the bag looks at me. Then they look at her.

"So you did know her," they say. "I didn't. But she was near the river. She could have drowned."

Who the hell knows the truth?

At least we found her.

CHAPTER 30

HONESTLY, I DON'T think that Gabe, Cedric, and I are heroes. I think we are just three kids who pretended to be real detectives, and then we got lucky—so we are sure not expecting a parade or a testimonial dinner. But the way the cops and detectives and grown-ups from the area are slapping our backs and high-fiving us, you'd think we'd just come back to Earth from a walk on Mars. We were just over-the-moon happy that we found that little girl.

I'm totally bad at guessing people's ages, but the

pretty woman carrying and kissing Yo-Yo looks like she's in her twenties. She's wearing a cleaning person's uniform. The sister we saw earlier is hanging close by her side. I can see from here both have been crying. It must be Yo-Yo's mom and sister. People just assumed the mom was a druggie or a jerk or both. Wow, were they ever wrong. Now I'm watching her and thinking she's just another mom who's trying to balance impossible things like jobs and kids and money and school.

But there is one thing I'm just never going to get away from.

"Hey," says one officer in uniform. "I hope you're bringing that smart brain of yours to that big debate."

Oh, yeah. The debate. It's been about fifteen minutes since somebody mentioned it. That's some kind of record, I think.

Then another officer says, "We're counting on you to change some minds, young man."

"Well, you'd better prepare yourself for some disappointment," Gabe says under his breath so only

I can hear. As always, he cracks himself up over his bad joke.

But most people are looking at us like a bunch of heroes.

It seems like everyone in the park wants to slap our backs or shake our hands. Even the pair of officers putting cuffs on the unhoused person give us a grateful nod.

Then comes the best part.

The woman carrying Yo-Yo and holding the big sister's hand walks toward us. With them is a whole group of friends, some laughing and crying all at once.

"I can't ever thank you guys enough," the mother says. "But I'm gonna try. Thank you. Thank you. Thank you. And God bless you." She keeps talking. Then, of course, she starts crying. I feel like I could start crying, too.

"Liana here was so tired from watching Yo-Yo last night when I was working that she fell asleep," Yo-Yo's mother says, as she puts her arm around the older sister.

Now I can't help wondering why the first officer we spoke to said that the big sister was on something. This girl is clearly just a kid, like us. Why are some people always ready to think the worst of one another? Sometimes this "detective's son" thinks the opposing debate rep has a good point or two.

Back to the scene at hand.

Yo-Yo's mother says, "But we sure did get a happy ending."

I suddenly hear another voice, a deeper voice, say, "Yes, ma'am, you certainly did."

God, I know that voice well, extremely well, too well.

It's my dad.

And, yes, of course I'm sure he's glad it ended happily, and I hope he's proud of me and my friends. But I also know that he is *not* happy that I lied to Nana Mama about going somewhere safe.

The same folks who were shaking my hand and high-fiving me are now shaking my dad's hand and giving him hugs. Finally everything seems to go quiet. The lost girl's mom says she's going to make me and my friends a special dinner sometime. Then my dad turns to me.

"Ali, how about you and I drive on home?"

I look up at my father.

"Serious car conversation coming up, Dad?" I ask. He pauses. Then he speaks.

"Let's call it semi-serious."

CHAPTER 31

THE CAR CONVERSATION stays calm. It could have been a lot worse. But even so, I'd think we could let punishment slide since I found the missing girl. Dad has a different opinion.

"We need some thoughtful discipline here, Ali," is what Dad says during the drive when I change from a big-deal hero into a little punk kid. "That's why I think grounding you is appropriate. Like I said, 'thoughtful.'"

"What makes discipline 'thoughtful'?" I ask him.

"Well, it creates an atmosphere where the person being disciplined can reflect upon the deed."

"I've reflected on it," I say. "There's not a lot more to think about."

"Yes, well, I'm sure you did think about it. But this will give you yet a little more time to reflect," he says.

"But, Dad, we were helping the police. We were helping the community. And best of all, we found the little girl."

For a moment I think he might be buying my argument. But then…

"Yes, you ended up doing something mighty good, but you began it by lying to your Nana, and the situation you jumped into was dangerous and unnecessary. You could have gotten hurt. There's a reason they don't have child cops."

Wow. That one hurts. Child? I bite my tongue, but this "child" ended up being better than the cops.

So, I'm grounded, for a whole week, starting the next day. It's not that I don't know the routine. I've been here before: I come home immediately after school ("No dawdling," according to Nana Mama, the warden), and, as you might have guessed, I can't go anywhere. No friends. No basketball. Nothing.

Look. I guess I understand it, but it sucks.

It lets me get my homework out of the way, but as soon as the homework is done, I start thinking about breaking one of the major "You're grounded" rules. That's the Alex Cross clause that states, "No cell phones except for absolute emergencies." Hmmm. Okay. My first day grounded. Gotta stay strong.

One good thing about being home is I can enjoy the sweet scent of the supper that Nana's starting to fix. I'm picking up the smell of onions, apples, and cinnamon. I gotta go check this out. I also want to tell her my version of what happened down at the Anacostia, since she probably only knows the follow-up from my dad: getting grounded. Damn.

I run down the stairs. I can hear the television playing in the living room. (Nana Mama is just about the only person I know who still gets her news from the TV.) I look in, expecting to find her sitting with a teacup in her hand and her eyes fixed on the screen.

No Nana Mama. But there is some guy on TV reading the local news.

"While it is clear that Detective Alex Cross did not participate in the actual shooting—he did not fire a gun—he remains a symbol of what troubles many citizens about dangerous police behavior. 'Slow to respond, quick to shoot,' as one Southeast mother put it."

The newscaster keeps talking about the shooting, about the police, about protesters. Then he lets go a piece of information that completely shocks me.

There's a huge anti-police protest at...the police station itself. The actual police station!

I run into the kitchen. Nana Mama is arranging apple slices in a pie shell.

"Well, well..." she begins saying. "Look who's..."

"Nana. Can't talk. I've got to go somewhere."

I'm at the kitchen door.

"Ali, you just hold on. You're—" she shouts.

"Sorry, gotta go."

And I'm gone.

CHAPTER 32

BEFORE I EVEN get over to the police station, my phone is spitting out alerts about the protest. Then I see it all for myself.

The guy on television called it a "significant disturbance." I'd call it something close to a riot. It's a really loud protest against police violence, police brutality, even the police in general. The crowd looks twice as big as the crowd that showed up outside our house. We could use Nana Mama to cool down this very angry bunch.

Cell phones are recording all over the place. News cameras and boom mics are set up toward the front of the crowd.

Signs are shaking in the air. Somehow, someone has managed to string a huge white bedsheet from the roof of the police station. On the bedsheet is the following order:

DEFUND THE POLICE NOW!!!

Four other people are struggling to keep a steady hold on another bedsheet banner.

STOP THE VIOLENCE! CUT THE BACON!

Among the crowd are children and teens and lots of grown-ups. Almost all the protesters are Black. A few white folks are standing here and there. These white people are just as angry and passionate as all the others.

I stand toward the edge of the crowd.

A chant builds. Loud. Louder. Loudest.

WE WANT THE CHIEF!

WE WANT THE CHIEF!

WE WANT THE CHIEF!

The front doors of the police station open. Four uniformed police officers step out. Two of the officers are Black. The other two are white. I've got to think that this is totally deliberate. And one of the white officers is a woman. Not just deliberate planning. *Political* planning.

WE WANT THE CHIEF!

WE WANT THE CHIEF!

WE WANT THE CHIEF!

Someone in charge inside must have decided that the only way to simmer this crowd down is to give them what they're screaming for.

Out walks Police Chief Gordon Dean Benton, a very tall, hulking guy who came up through the ranks and is about as well-liked as anybody in that job can be. Benton always enjoys the spotlight, and he seems to be on the local stations every other day. He's a smooth talker. I suddenly remember my dad saying, *Gordy Benton has been running for office since he was in kindergarten.*

Chief Benton starts talking, and from the get-go

it sounds like he copied his "impromptu remarks" out of a grammar school civics book from a hundred years ago.

"Trying to defend civil liberty and the citizens themselves is a great challenge."

Man. I can immediately tell this is not going to end well.

"The job that the police have to do and the will of the people must be joined together."

Someone from the crowd yells, "Kill the cops before they kill more of us." This sounds a little harsh to me, but so many other people join in with "Yeah" or "Amen" or "Say it."

Benton just keeps on yapping.

"I appreciate the will of the people, but I also appreciate the task of the police."

A tall Black man standing next to me holds a megaphone to his mouth and begins yelling.

"Lies. Lies. Lies." He says it over and over. He's practically chanting the words. Because of this guy, lots of people in the crowd—and their cameras—turn toward us. Some of them say, "Yessir, brother" and others say, "Let the man talk." Whatever—they're looking at the guy with the megaphone. But, of course, they can't help but notice me.

I scan the faces looking over at me. And I suddenly see a face I absolutely do not want to see.

Yeah, you guessed it.

Detective Alex Cross.

Our eyes meet. I'm scared. I'm nervous. I should be home doing homework. I should be grounded. I should be anywhere but here.

Then my dad nods his head. He nods it twice. Three times.

Okay. I got it.

This place is important. This event is important.

I know I'm right about this. My dad is cool that I'm here.

CHAPTER 33

THE GOOD NEWS is that the demonstration eventually calms down. Not because of the totally weak-ass speech that the police chief gives. Like the woman next to me says, "I sure hope the chief doesn't hurt himself trying to sit on both sides of the fence at the same time."

One of the group leaders, a young woman who introduces herself as the author of a book called *Politics, Peace, and Promise,* gives a speech to the crowd. She tells them there'll be a committee meeting tomorrow at the town recreation center on Holfield Street. When she reminds the group that this is "only the beginning of our story, not the end of it," everyone seems to calm down a little. Besides, even the most passionate people have chores to do and jobs to get to and suppers to eat.

Like I said, that's the good news.

The bad news? The bad news only applies to me: I'd broken the rules of my grounding.

My dad says he was happy I got to see the passion that people have about the issue that I'm about to debate. But he also says that he can't ignore the fact that I had disobeyed him.

His parting words? "Grounded means grounded. It's as simple as that."

I think maybe the worst part of being grounded is not just having to stay inside my house all the time but also having to stay inside my house *without having any of my friends over.* Yeah, sure, we text until our thumbs are practically bloody (when I get to use my phone, at least), but it's not the same as having the guys right there.

That's the reason I practically fall over when

Nana Mama shouts up the stairs on the second day of my punishment, "Ali, there's a friend of yours down here who wants to see you!"

This is highly suspicious.

Nana is the person my dad counts on to make sure I'm not breaking any of the grounding rules, and there's no arguing with Nana Mama when she's the warden. She would have handed me my behind for walking out of here the other day, except Dad got to me first.

When Nana's on watch duty, Gabe and Cedric and Mateo don't even bother trying to make it inside the house. Their usual approach—lines like "I just need to ask Ali some questions about the math homework" or "It'll only take a second"—just won't work.

But Nana Mama is no fool. She knows we all basically live on our phones. She'll just say to my friends, *Well, if you need math homework or you need Ali for just a second, give him a yell on one of your phones. They're very helpful devices. That's why people call 'em "smartphones."*

So, thinking about that, I'm a little confused

when she tells me about a "friend of yours down here who wants to see you." Not just confused. I'm confused and super curious.

I run down the stairs. I run into the kitchen. And there's Nana Mama standing pouring a cup of coffee for my dad's best friend, John Sampson.

Hey, it's not that I'm disappointed. Sampson is my friend, too. He's also a fun guy, a grown-up I'm usually really happy to hang with. But...well, I've got to admit it. I was hoping for Cedric or Gabe.

Sampson and I give each other a hug. Of course, he squeezes hard enough that I think my ears might fly off. (Why do some old guys do that?)

"Don't pretend you're happy to see me, Ali. My guess is that you were hoping for a friend about thirty years younger," he says.

"No, it's not that— It's just that—" I stammer like a fool. Detective Sampson tries to help me out.

"Ali, I'd feel the exact same way. But would it interest you to know that I'm actually here on official business?" he asks.

Nana is making herself some hot water with lemon. She's not even paying attention to our conversation, or at least she's pretending not to. Well, Sampson's visit can't be about anything serious or Nana would be all over it. Anyway, I'm wondering what makes the detective's business "official."

So, think about it. When I walked into the kitchen and saw that John Sampson was my visitor, at first I thought he was here for some horrible scary reason. Right now, I make a total about-face, and I'm thinking he might be here to present me and my friends with some sort of official police commendation for helping find that girl. Wait. Did I say *helping* find that girl? Man, we found her. Bring on the commendation.

"Does this have to do with finding the lost child down by the river?" I ask. I'm pretty sure now that this is going to be a big-deal thank-you. But—hey, wait a second—where's the mayor? Where's the little girl? Where's the band? Where's the cake?

"Yes, sir," Detective Sampson says. "It is connected with the exceptional assistance you gave all of us in the MPD."

Then he explains a little more, and, not to jump

ahead, but now we come to the part where I feel like a total fool, a total fool who's been brought down a peg or two.

Sampson explains.

"The officers on the scene where you and your friends exhibited such bravery did not have the opportunity to complete a full and comprehensive interview. When your dad heard that we had to do a follow-up, he suggested to the chief that he'd rather not have you come down to the station house. So that son-of-a-gun Alex volunteered me to come out and do the interview for the record."

There's a pause. Then Detective Sampson says, with a very small smile, "Your dad seemed pretty certain that I'd find you home."

My dad was "pretty certain" that John Sampson would find me at home? Very funny. A "grounded" joke.

As Nana Mama leaves the kitchen with her hot water and lemon she says, "Well, I'll leave you men alone. Call me if you need anything. And by the way, there are four marshmallow brownies hidden on the second pantry shelf behind the baked beans. Enjoy them."

John Sampson takes out his laptop and logs on. Then he pauses again, and sort of stares off into space.

"Okay, Detective, we can get started," I say. But Detective Sampson is still just gazing off into space. Then he looks at me and raises his eyebrows.

"You waiting for your computer to load?" I ask.

"No, man," he says. "I'm waiting for you to get us those brownies."

Chapter 34

So we begin.

Most of the "interview" questions are kind of boring, but I really do appreciate the fact that my dad's best friend took the trouble to come out to our house to do it in person.

Some of the questions are questions Detective Sampson could have answered himself (although I do a great job giving my name, address, date of birth, and where I go to school).

Some of the questions I just don't have an answer for.

Question: "How many police officers escorted you and your friends during your investigation at the shore of the Anacostia River?"

Answer: "Huh? One, five, ten, I don't know."

Some of the questions are slightly confusing.

Question: "How would you describe the man who was holding the victim?"

Answer: "Huh again? Didn't they arrest the guy and bring him down to the station? Don't they already know what he looks like?"

Anyway, the whole interview takes about a half hour, and Detective Sampson agrees that some of the stuff he has to ask was a little foolish, but he also says that accuracy and fairness are "imperative in the pursuit of justice." I tell him that I absolutely agree, and who am I to stand in the way of the pursuit of justice?

As I expected, Detective Sampson is really nice about everything. And Nana Mama's marshmallow brownies help the situation a lot. Detective Sampson keeps asking me if I'm nervous. Do I want to take a break? Do I need to go to the bathroom? Do I want half of his second brownie?

And so we finish the interview. And we also finish the brownies. But Detective Sampson makes no move to get up from the kitchen table and leave. This is fine with me because I was expecting something more interesting than the boring interview, and I really like John Sampson, and, not to be obsessive about the brownies, but...if Nana Mama gave us four brownies, there's got to be a lot more left somewhere in the baking pan. I'm hoping, of course, that he'll be willing to discuss some interesting cases he's working on. I'm hoping he'll spill some gossip about who's doing what down at the station. I'm even hoping that he'll forget who he's talking to, and tell me something I don't know about my dad and his job.

That's not what happens.

As I'm considering all this, Detective Sampson says, "Ali, there is a whole other reason why I wanted to come here and talk to you today in private. And it's a fairly serious one."

When I hear him say "serious" I get scared. Really

scared. He sounds like he's about to break some bad news.

Who's dead? Who's sick? Who's almost dead? Who's been fired? Who's in trouble?

Oh, shit, man. Jannie? Gabe? My dad?

My brain is going wild with horrible ideas.

"Here's what I want to talk to you about, Ali."

Hurry the hell up, Detective Sampson. I think I may have to go to the bathroom.

"Our police communications officers have detected that someone has been using a custom-designed smartphone application to intercept and transcribe DC Metro Police emergency radio transmissions," he says. "We traced the cell numbers. And one of them... belongs to you."

He pauses. I'm not sure if he's waiting for me to confirm or deny his statement, but all I can think is...I'm going to jail...or reform school... or what I've heard some guys in school call "baby prison."

Then Detective Sampson says, "I'm right about this. Aren't I, Ali?" I freeze—not on purpose—for a few seconds, or maybe even a few minutes.

But, hey, there is absolutely no point in lying (although I actually do consider doing that).

"Yes, sir," I say. There's nothing else for me to say.

"I'm sure it crossed your mind that police scanner apps aren't, oh, let's say, legal?"

"Uh, well, we thought that...maybe..." I say. "But..." I stop talking.

But not talking is no problem; Detective Sampson finishes the sentence for me.

"But you thought you would never get caught," he says.

Of course, he's right. He knows that. And I know that.

"Listen, you guys are not the first ones to do this, but here's the deal. STOP IT!"

And just in case I didn't realize that he was really pissed, he says, "And I mean that. You jokers have to stop it right now."

He knows he's made his point. I'm spooked enough by his "police voice"; I'm used to a much goofier Detective Sampson, one who likes to joke around.

"At the moment we'll consider this whole thing

private information just between you and me," he says.

"So my dad doesn't know?" I ask, my voice cracking, my stomach jumping.

"Your dad has got enough on his mind. So, no, I haven't shared this with him, and I don't plan to... IF YOU STOP DOING IT NOW."

"Yes, this isn't something we should bother him with," I say. "My dad is busy right now. Really busy."

Sampson nods in agreement and says, "Yeah, I'm sure that was weighing on your mind."

I stare at the floor with a look that I hope says, "I'm sorry for being a fool." I should just shut up and stop while I'm ahead. But now I can't resist asking just one more question.

"So I'm not going to jail?"

"Not this time," he says. I'm waiting for a friendly smile.

It doesn't come.

Chapter 35

I TELL GABE what John Sampson told me, that he knows what we've been up to. Gabe's initial reaction is exactly like mine: total fear. "Ali, can we get in trouble for this?"

"We're really lucky," I tell him. "We got off with a warning this time." As soon as Gabe hears this, he is completely relieved.

Not me. I cannot calm down. I mean, after all, I'm the cop kid. I'm the policeman's son. I came *this* close to living the nightmare. Plus I know that if my dad ever finds out what happened, he'd be more than *angry.* He'd be the worst thing of all—*disappointed.*

So I carry a whole lot of nervous brain and rumbling belly around with me the rest of the day. At supper, I can only force down two slices of Nana Mama's banana pound cake.

Anyway, here it is, nine o'clock at night on what should have been an ordinary Wednesday (but isn't).

Okay, it looks normal enough. My homework is done. Dad is at work. I've read my debate notes so many times that I think I've actually memorized all the statistics and quotations. Between thinking about the debate and worrying about Dad finding out about our "intercepting" crime, I'm not doing well at all.

I go downstairs and watch Bree play a game on her laptop. (I'd love to play, too, but can't use my phone until my grounding's up.) A few nights ago, I taught her how to play *Among Us.* The lady is not just a powerhouse in the game. She's also become pretty much an *Among Us* fanatic.

Here's proof. At nine thirty, when Nana Mama comes into the dining room and says it's time for bed, Bree—a senior detective, a courageous police officer, not to mention a wicked-good stepmother—says exactly what I usually say: "Oh, please Nana, just ten more minutes."

Nana gives us the ten minutes, and then I'm up the stairs. Teeth brushed. Earbuds in place to listen to blink-182. Lights out. I gotta hit the peaceful button inside myself so I don't hit the snooze tomorrow.

But then the debate invades my brain. The debate...the debate...the debate....Damn. Where has that nightmare been hiding the past hour? Congratulations to Nana Mama's fine cooking and that fine game for making me forget a little bit. But those few hours of peace are all in the past. Now I'm wide awake and dancing with the thought of the packed auditorium, the parents, the kids, the police, the demonstrations.

I hear the music in my earbuds, but I'm only thinking about the debate.

I pull out the earbuds and pull open my laptop.

Twenty-five pages of debate notes, everything from information about the first US police force (New York City, 1846) to an article about "Brute Force in Blue" (University of Dayton Publishing). Yes, I have memorized it all. But reading it again won't hurt. At some point, I fall asleep.

I'm sleeping with my laptop open when a loud, dinging alert from Gabe's app startles me awake. My phone says 2:10 a.m. What the hell? How's that possible? Gabe was supposed to disconnect the system hours ago. Instead I'm reading about a violent incident with possible firearms at 133 Bangor Street Southeast.

I text: R u serious? kill system now

Gabe texts: not sure it's actually illegal

Then he texts again: Besides, 2 good 2 pass on this one

I text: ur going to jail alone

Gabe does not text back. Instead he actually calls.

"Come on, Ali. One last adventure. Then I'll destroy the whole setup. I promise. Let's do it," he says.

"No way. Our one last adventure is going to get

us arrested, 'cause we were too stupid to take a favor from John Sampson," I say.

"Listen, if there's a problem, we tell Detective Sampson that we tried to disable the app, but..."

"You know, for a genius, you make really bad decisions. No."

"You know, for a police detective, you're pretty chicken," he says.

I hang up. I rub my eyes. If Sampson finds out, if my dad finds out...plus, there's the debate...

I promised Detective Sampson we'd stop. I can't give in. Damn. I...will...not...give...in.

Then Gabe's phrase races through my brain. "You're pretty chicken."

Maybe I should reconsider. After all, Gabe did promise that after this last crime scene he would "destroy the whole setup." This would be one last adventure.

Okay. The farewell tour.

Maybe. I think. I won't. I will.

I trade my old T-shirt for a denim collared shirt. I jump into a pair of cargo shorts. Closest-to-the-bed sneakers will do. Wallet. Keys. Phone.

And suddenly, I just can't move.

My feet won't hold me up. My legs won't start. One simple job to do—walk. Yeah, I know how to walk, but I can't. Every once in a while, I've got to follow the rules. Damn. This is one of those times.

I text Gabe: **Can't do it, man. Talk later.**

Gabe texts me: **Don't freak, dude. Just don't let me down tomorrow.**

I lay my head back on the pillow. I know I'm not going to fall asleep soon. So, of course, there's only one thing left to do. I think about the debate.

The debate. The debate. The debate.

Chapter 36

THIS IS THE most important event of my life so far.

Here I am at Nationals Park, about to pitch the last ball in the last game of the World Series.

Okay. Just joking. In case you didn't guess.

Here I am, center stage at Madison Square Garden, about to perform with Beyoncé and Jay-Z.

Okay. Joking again.

But you get it. This is important, and I'm scared. Very scared. Whatever that land beyond "scared" is, that's the land I'm living in.

This is debate day.

Sienna and I are standing at two scratched-up wobbly wooden podiums on the auditorium stage. Even though the middle school auditorium only holds two hundred people, tops, it looks like they've managed to pack the place with a hundred more. Some grown-ups are sitting on the floor. Lots of people are standing in the back. Kids are packed into the bleachers. Great. The bleachers give Sienna's fans more room to hold up banners that say things like AND THE WINNER IS SIENNA and YOU GO, SIENNA. There are a few signs apparently left over from some of the demonstrations. To the near right of me I read FRY THE PIG spray-painted on a sheet. A teacher makes those kids take it down. But it's tense.

Oh, sure, I've got my team. But it really isn't a big team. Up in the bleachers are Cedric, Mateo, Gabe, and maybe five other kids I know, all seated together.

Who else is there for me? Of course Nana Mama and Bree and Jannie and Detective Sampson. Dad is missing in action, that action being a narcotics recovery board meeting with some big shots over at George Washington University.

But the school auditorium is still standing-room only. Different teachers seem to be huddled together. And, of course, the place is peppered with the local leaders—the police chief, the police commissioner, the owner of the sporting goods store, two Baptist ministers, a lot of police officers, and… well, it's crowded.

Suddenly, just as I start to get used to the big crowd, I'm not so scared about the debate itself. That doesn't mean I'm feeling great, though. I wish to hell I'd stop sweating, stop squinting, stop touching my hair. Why do I keep smoothing my hair on top? Why am I pulling up my socks? Why does my throat feel so scratchy? Now I just hope I don't throw up or trip or use the same chop-the-air hand gesture too much. I also wish that someone hadn't carved "LOSER" into the top of my podium.

Of course, Sienna looks great, like she's about to give a tough TV interview to some nasty senator. Black pants, dark gray sweater, a gold chain with a dangling gold cross. (A cross? Isn't that cheating?)

Me, I'm dressed like a nerd from Planet Loser. Nana Mama said that my regular jeans were "too tight for standing on a stage," so I ended up in my go-to church khakis. Nana's fashion advice was also to "wear a collared shirt," which meant I shouldn't wear a T-shirt. So Sienna is standing up here looking like a celebrity, and I'm standing a few feet away from her looking like a kid who's late for bio class.

It's only been about fifteen seconds that my opponent and I have been standing here, but when Ms. Swanbeck, the debate moderator, starts walking down the aisle, I feel like I've actually been waiting for a few days.

Ms. Swanbeck steps to the center of the stage, and it's at just that moment that Cedric and Gabe decide to shout out, "Go Ali!" This gets an immediate response from a lot of the crowd—a huge, loud chorus of boos. The guys couldn't have waited, huh? They just couldn't have waited.

Ms. Swanbeck speaks. "Let's everybody stay calm. A friendly and fair debate. Isn't that what we all want?"

Uh, yeah. I guess.

But you know what I want most of all?

I just want it to be over.

CHAPTER 37

MS. SWANBECK SAYS, "Let's get started, shall we? Are the debaters ready?"

"Yes, I'm ready," I say.

"Yes, ma'am," Sienna says.

I don't have time to think about the fact that using the super-respectful "ma'am" puts Sienna ahead of me already. Ms. Swanbeck hits a button on her laptop, and the theme of the debate flashes on the screen behind Sienna and me.

THE DC POLICE
PART OF THE PROBLEM?
PART OF THE SOLUTION?
OR BOTH?

Coin toss. Sienna wins the toss and chooses to go first. And, damn, she is just like a TV personality. So cool. So calm. She's not only got a sweet, sincere smile, but when she starts talking, well, she's prepared. She's got the cold hard facts to go with her look.

Smooth, confident, she talks to the audience like she's talking to her best friend.

"The actual statistics speak to the real root of the problem. In areas of Southeast where, as we all know, the population is predominantly Black, the police officers assigned to it are"—Sienna pauses, a smart move on her part—"predominantly white. Just in this ten-block area, this area right here, surrounding this school, the neighborhood is 68 percent people of color. Yet according to public records, assigned police officers are only 35 percent Black. C'mon, people. Racist white police..."

I interrupt. I have to. "Hold on. Racist? How do you know these officers are ra—"

Ms. Swanbeck steps in. "Please, Ali. Let Sienna continue. You'll have your time very soon. Continue, Sienna."

She does. And wow is she clever.

"I think Ali has a good point. I think using the word *racist* is prejudicial. I retract it."

Okay, she's cemented the word *racist* by saying it twice, and now she sounds better than ever by apologizing for using it.

She continues.

"Yes, let's deal only in facts. Here's one. Last summer, during the months of June, July, and August, twenty-two police officers were brought up before the review board on brutality and abuse charges. Do you know how many of those twenty-two were further investigated?"

A voice from the audience. "Probably none of them."

Sienna says, "You're close, Leonard." Ah, using the personal touch.

"But the accurate answer is 'one.' Yeah, that's right.

Of all those cops accused, only one went beyond the police review board to an actual court hearing. And, oh, by the way, that one cop was found not guilty."

Cries of "Go, Sienna" and "You're right, girl" and "Forget the cops" fill the huge room.

Ms. Swanbeck steps forward quick and tells the audience to calm down. Once they do, she can't resist giving a short lecture.

"This is meant to be a civilized discussion of ideas." Then she looks at me and says, "So, Ali, would you like to respond to Sienna's comments?"

What the hell is Swanbeck expecting me to say? Uh, no—let's end it here?

I squeeze my eyes shut, just for a second, but in that second, I decide exactly what I should say. I've learned a lesson from Sienna, but I'm going to be flying way higher, and I'm going to touch the freaking sky.

Damn. I know what I'm doing! I open my eyes real wide, and I speak.

"Sienna, I completely agree with you."

Huge pause.

I wouldn't say that the crowd actually gasps, but

there's conversation and murmuring, and I can actually hear some kid say, "Ali's gotta be crazy, man."

I quickly glance around at the crowd, and see that Nana Mama and Cedric—sitting far away from one another—have the very same tiny little grins on their faces. They are the two folks out there who know me well enough to realize exactly what kinda mischief I'm up to.

"Yes, I do agree with you, Sienna. The situation is absolutely reprehensible." I had been saving that word, *reprehensible*, for just the right moment.

I plow ahead. Not excessive or overdoing anything, just moving along with a little speed.

"Sure, there are police officers who don't do right by the neighborhood, officers who use violent tactics. And no one—least of all me, a kid who's grown up with police in my house, in my family—is going to say they shouldn't be totally investigated and brought up on charges. And if they're guilty, charge them. But—and this is the major difference between you and me and some of the people in this room—the people who are committing the crimes, the folks doing the bad things, well, they also have got to be stopped. They *should* be stopped. And the people those folks are hurting? Well, they should be helped. And that's what hundreds of fine officers do. We can talk all day about why the crime is happening—poverty, drugs, frustration—but, ladies and gentlemen, this life, this neighborhood, this here is a two-way street."

CHAPTER 38

I REALLY WISH I could say that everybody is now standing up and cheering.

No. But...I'm just happy that nobody is hissing and booing.

Nana Mama and Bree and Detective Sampson and Cedric and Mateo and Gabe do start to applaud, and I admit that it sounds pretty pathetic. Then a few more people join in. They actually may be people I don't know. So that's good. It's the kind of applause that I think could be called "respectable."

And to me "respectable" is at least preferable to "embarrassing."

What's even better is that I see a few faces that are not members of my fan club, kids who were at the anti-police demonstrations, who remain seated but are clapping. Some of them even shoot some peaceful nods toward me.

Armed with a bunch of solid facts, and inspired by the enthusiasm of the crowd, Sienna and I volley pretty strongly. I like to think that it never turns nasty because we're friends, but the truth is we're both too smart to let that happen.

Five minutes more. Ten minutes more. I play the interviews Gabe and I filmed of people talking about how the police helped them. I think we're both relieved when Ms. Swanbeck steps forward and says something like, "Well, okay. Why don't we ask Sienna and Ali to join the debate team?"

Then Ms. Swanbeck introduces Ms. Garrity, the assistant principal, who tells us that "we all learned a great deal today."

Some girl yells out, "Yeah, for a change."

Of course, everyone hoots, cheers, and laughs.

"Food for thought. Food for thought," Ms. Garrity says. "Thanks for joining us, everyone."

I'm not sure whether any of us knows if we're supposed to go to homeroom or our next class. But it's close enough to the end of school that I don't think anybody's going anywhere except outside.

I'm about to step down off the stage when Sienna calls to me.

"Wait up, Ali," she says as she walks toward me. I'm thinking that this girl hasn't spoken a word to me in days. And she's not looking too friendly right now. What's up?

"Nice job, Ali," she says. "Really smooth curveball you tossed."

"Thanks," I say. And I mean it when I say, "Very nice job from you, too."

No, she does not lean in and give me a hug. But she does put her hand out for a shake. And that's almost as good.

Then my family and a few friends join us. Sienna steps away to join her own crowd of friends and fans.

"Eloquent," says Nana Mama. "Eloquent. That's what you were."

My friend Gabe congratulates me in his own special way. "Hey, really good debate. Exactly what we expected from two nerd-balls like Sienna and you."

Then I hear someone say, "Nerd-ball or not, I thought you were terrific."

It's my dad.

He hugs me hard.

"I snuck in from the side door. After all, I didn't want to make you nervous, and I certainly didn't want anyone in the audience to see your father, 'the cop.' "

CHAPTER 39

MY FAMILY AND I walk home from the debate. Of course, I'm sweaty and thirsty and hungry. And I'm looking forward to cracking open a can of cold soda and chowing down on some leftovers.

But I should have known. Nana Mama doesn't let any occasion go by without some good food. And I guess that—win or lose—she planned on treating the debate as a special event.

And there it is, all laid out on the dining room table, a help-yourself buffet set with cloth napkins and Sunday china. I've seen it all before, and I couldn't be happier about it. This is what Nana Mama calls her "High-Style Wedding, Baptism, and Funeral Spread." A big bowl of shrimp with mustard-mayo dipping sauce, a platter of ham biscuits, a corn-and-sugar-bean salad. And what would Nana's High-Style Spread be without Nana's coconut cream cake?

After I tell Nana Mama how incredible, unbelievable, and really, really appreciated this is, I yell, "Don't anybody touch anything."

I take a few pics of the spread, focusing heavily on the big bowl of shrimp. Shrimp is considered a semi-luxury in the Cross house. And it's nothing for Jannie and me to vacuum up an entire bowl of the little critters like popcorn.

Dad sounds the warning. "Make sure everybody gets their fair share of shrimp. And this advice is especially pertinent to our champion debater."

Jannie apparently decides to ignore Dad's message and begins scooping the shrimp onto her plate like...well, like popcorn.

Usually I would yell out something like, "Dad, Jannie's not obeying. Look at all she took."

But, for some reason I can't explain at all, I decide to keep quiet. In fact, there's something nice about watching Jannie enjoy herself. Let her have fun. Yeah, that's what I'm thinking.

Thing is, I don't know why I'm feeling this way. I don't think it's a sudden kind of grown-up maturity from doing a good job at the debate. Really, I don't feel any emotion other than relief that the damn thing is over. And that feeling is totally not surprising.

But I think I'm also glad that, even though no one technically "won" the debate, a conversation was started. And we all came together.

Whatever. I'd better stop this deep thinking and dive into the shrimp before Jannie goes back for seconds.

We all fill our plates, and before we begin eating, Dad raises his glass of seltzer, no ice ("it breaks up the bubbles").

"To Ali. Who spoke the truth. And maybe taught some people that the truth can be pretty complicated."

Then Bree says, "And, in fairness, I say we raise

a toast in honor of the young woman who represented the other side of the debate. To..."

Bree stumbles just for a moment, so Jannie chimes in.

"Sienna," Jannie says.

There is a silence that lasts a few seconds. Of course, Bree and Dad and Nana Mama exchange those obnoxious all-knowing looks that adults often give.

Then Bree speaks directly to me.

"Do you know Sienna well, Ali?" she asks.

Then Jannie goes, "*Yeah,* Ali, do you know Sienna well?"

I suddenly regret letting her get away with taking all those shrimp.

Here's how the conversation goes.

"These ham biscuits are really delicious, Nana," I say.

Pause. Then I turn to Bree and speak.

"I'm sorry, Bree. What was it you were asking?"

The shrimp bowl goes empty. Only two biscuits remain. They'll be put to bed in Tupperware. The corn salad did well for itself, considering it was a vegetable. And the cake. What we didn't finish at this meal we'll eat later on while we're watching clips from last week's John Oliver.

We all help clear the table, and I slip on Nana's baby-blue rubber gloves to start washing the dishes.

"I'll take care of those dishes and forks, Ali," Nana says. "You had a big day. Go on up to your room and start your homework."

Dad is putting on his light raincoat. He's told us he's going to ride with three officers who are trying to nab some of the "professional" shoplifters who have been invading CVS and Walgreens.

"But, Nana," Dad says. "Ali can do the dishes. The boy has unlimited amounts of energy. Just hand him the sponge."

"Jannie also has unlimited energy. Tell her to lend a hand," I say. My sweet patience and understanding for my sister was short-lived.

Dad leaves. And I—champion debater, hero, Wonder Boy—I plunge my hands into the hot greasy dishwater.

CHAPTER 40

I'M UPSTAIRS IN my bedroom. And I guess I'm pretty calm. And I guess I'm pretty happy. But I've got to say that it's a nervous calm, a nervous happy. I'm still buzzing from the debate.

(Duh. You think so, Ali?)

I know I could just pass out in a few minutes because I'm so tired, or I might still be so buzzed from the overwhelming day that I'll still be awake to see the sunrise over our next-door neighbor's garage.

I can't really concentrate on homework. So I do just the stuff that absolutely must be turned in tomorrow. Then I spend about five minutes on my laptop with a video game. (*Blasters of the Universe.* I don't recommend it.) Then, a really tiny chore: I'm not a real good clothes-folder, but I do my best folding job just to get those stupid khaki pants out of my sight.

Then…I'm asleep.

I don't remember falling asleep. But when my cell phone rings and I open my eyes, I realize that I'm still wearing my jeans and T-shirt from earlier. The phone tells me the time: 1:25 a.m. I hear Gabe's very excited voice.

"Hey, dude. There's heavy police action just around the corner from you. 1411 U Street. I got the info."

"Wait a minute, Gabe. Last night, you promised you were going to shut down the app after…"

"I did. I did. And I shut it down. Honest. But then I messed around and figured out a way to bring it back online without getting caught," he says.

"What is wrong with you, dude? We could…"

"Not 'we.' Just me. I didn't install it on your phone. So don't worry. But it's working great. That's how I got this news about the scene on U Street."

I do know exactly where that is. Incredible, really. And yes, it is just around the block from our house. I also know exactly why the address is so familiar. It's where Bree and Dad's friends, DeeDee and Randy Pearson, live.

"Listen, Ali. Here goes," Gabe says. And before I can even stop him, he rattles off the details on his screen.

domestic violence.

male possibly armed.

proceed with caution.

Now I'm not as upset about Gabe's bringing back the intercept system. I'm more worried about the fact that this report is about our friends the Pearsons.

I mean, get out of here. This can't be true at all. Talk about nice folks, upstanding citizens. Mrs. P is a school nurse up near Georgetown. Mr. P is a physician's assistant at Walter Reed hospital. No. Nothing wrong with the Pearsons. It's got to be some folks visiting the Pearsons. Or maybe worse. Intruders. Burglars. Robbers. Something like that.

I gotta go. And anyway, I didn't get the news on *my* phone. Gabe called me. And he said the new system had been perfected. And these are our friends. And it's around the corner. And I'll get Gabe to kill the system right after this one time. And... and... and I know I'm grounded. But I'm on it.

Since I'm already dressed, I'm set to go, an expert at sneaking out of my house.

Nana's door is closed. She must be sleeping. Dad and Bree's door is closed, and I don't think he's even home from his shoplifting investigation.

It turns out there is one mouse stirring: Jannie. I pass her at the kitchen table, most likely working on her overdue psych paper.

"Where are you sneaking off to?" she says as I head for the door.

I'm pushing my feet into my sneaks.

"Shush," I say. "I've got business."

"I'm sure."

"Don't tell anyone," I say.

"No one to tell," she says. "Dad is out doing his job. Bree turned in, and Nana is in..."

I'm already out the door, running down 15th Street toward U Street. Number 1411. I can make it there in less than two minutes.

CHAPTER 41

THE HOUSE ON 1411 U Street. The Pearson house. A small split-level. White aluminum siding. A red front door. Neat and tidy.

The upstairs lights are on. The downstairs lights are on. But that's it. No police. No sirens. No flashing lights. No nosy neighbors.

What's going on?

I text Gabe.

Am at crime scene. Nothing.

He texts back.

Ur there already wow. DCP on way. Stay cool.

Now I get it. I live so close that I beat the police to the location.

I study the house a little more carefully, and I get the feeling that something isn't quite right. It's not just all the bright indoor lighting. There's a big brown leather easy chair overturned on the front lawn toward the side of the house. In the tiny driveway, the side door on the passenger side of a Kia has been left open. Even that storybook red front door has been left open a crack. It seems maybe that someone was in a big rush to get inside or outside. I can't figure out which.

But I want to check it out. Just like a real detective would.

I slowly walk up to the house, when all of a sudden, I hear voices coming from inside. I can't understand a word of anything that's being said, but they're definitely voices. A radio? Someone on speakerphone? Whatever it is, they sound urgent. Not scared, just nervous.

Seconds after I hear those voices, I hear sirens. No one asked me, and I still have a lot to learn about police work, but screaming-loud sirens can't be a good idea. What if someone in the house is violent and dangerous? Then couldn't they become more scared and more anxious? Couldn't they end up doing something dangerous?

The first of three police cars screeches into the Pearsons' tiny driveway. The other two police cars park on the street. A fourth car shows up and puts itself smack on the small front lawn. Two ambulances—a fire department ambulance and a hospital ambulance—roar up, also with sirens screaming.

Then suddenly I hear, we all hear, the unmistakable explosion of gunfire.

One shot.

Two shots.

Three shots.

Men and women, officers and EMS workers, all rush from their vehicles. Some approach the house. Others start setting up roadblocks. They wrap yellow POLICE LINE DO NOT CROSS tape around trees and sawhorses.

I look at the crowd of police gathering. Six of them are in uniform. Three of them are in plain clothes.

And one of those plainclothes officers is my dad.

"Get the hell out of here, kid," another police officer hisses at me. I'm still on the street in front of the house, but close enough to see the action. "You wanna get killed?"

He's right. Maybe I could be killed.

My heart is pounding. My breathing is sharp, fast.

But I'm not going anywhere.

Not when my dad's life is *also* in danger.

I need to stay and see what happens.

When no one is looking, I run to the side of the house and stand on a strip of brown lawn near the driveway. I have a pretty good view of the front of the house, if I squat and lean forward a little. And I have a very clear view of the police and vehicles in the front of the house. Of course, the person I'm mostly concentrating on watching is my dad. Right now he's talking with two uniformed officers, a man and a woman, both of them armed.

There is a series of awful noises from the house. Three more gunshots.

The big glass picture window in the front of the house shatters and crumbles. All the police officers, including my dad and his two companions, drop to the ground.

It's at this moment that I see something that sends fear through my whole body. My dad squats close to the ground and begins to creep slowly toward the house.

I can see that he's holding a cell phone in his right hand. I'm so shaken with fear that I actually, really, absolutely think that I should scream at him to get the hell away from where he's crouching.

Then I hear his voice shouting to someone in the house. "Pick up your phone. Get on your phone."

Inside the house, I start to make out two figures. Familiar ones. I can see Randy approach some sort of table. DeeDee is near him, but I can't tell who is threatening whom. They both look terrified.

And so am I.

"Pick it up," my dad yells.

Then DeeDee shouts, "Go ahead. Pick up the damn phone."

Randy holds the phone to his ear. For me the whole

scene is one huge horror movie. Except here I am, an actual part of it.

I kneel and then crawl around. I find a spot where I think I won't be noticed, and I watch the floodlighted front lawn where the movie is unfolding. But this is no movie set. This is the very real little front lawn of a little house where my father has become the easy target of a bad guy with a gun.

I hear my dad's voice. He's not really shouting, but he's loud. Commanding. I don't know how he doesn't seem afraid.

"Pick up the cell phone, Randy. Pick it up. Talk to me," my dad says.

A woman's voice quickly follows. I have no trouble hearing her, either.

"Go ahead, Randy. Pick up the phone. Pick up the damn phone."

My dad keeps moving slowly toward the house. All the other police officers remain close to the sidewalk in front.

Dad stops moving. He holds the phone to his ear. He talks.

"Randy, can you hear me? Are you with me?"

My eyes are jumping back and forth between the broken window and my father. Randy Pearson does not answer my father's questions. For a moment, I survey the bigger scene near the sidewalk. There is a lot of quiet movement. I see officers and plain-clothes detectives moving across neighbors' lawns. I hear voices in loud whispers giving instructions.

"473 to house northwest."

"135 with Glock at barbecue setup."

"Check 496 and 553 on rear neighbor roof."

Then I hear my dad's voice. It's firm. No shaking, no nerves.

"It would be really great if you could throw your gun out the window, Randy. For your family, for your wife, for yourself."

Dad gets his answer.

A six-bullet volley of shots. Two or three of the bullets snap the bark off a skinny tree in the front yard. Lots of people drop flat to the ground. Even I duck automatically, holding my hands over my head. Not my dad. For the first time I notice that beneath his jacket, he's wearing a full-armor vest, neck level to below waist level.

"You're talkin' to the wrong person, Alex," I hear Mr. Pearson yell.

"No, my friend. I'm talkin' to you. There's no problem you're having that we cannot sort out," says my dad.

"Goddam it, Alex. You're wrong. You guys have it all wrong. My wife is the person shooting the gun."

Chapter 42

Sometimes, not a lot of times, my dad would tell me about some of the rough things he faced as a police detective. Yes, I'm sure he cleaned up his stories of the drug busts and the gang fights and the homicides he was involved in. But how many times did I think, how many times did I say, *I wish I could have been there*? How many times did I race to the scene of a call, hoping to see some action like this?

And now I am there. I'm actually there. Here.

And I'd rather be anyplace else in the world.

The police have cordoned off the scene. No curious neighbors. No "lookie-loos." No news cameras or reporters for blocks and blocks. Just cops and detectives and medics and firemen and my dad. My dad with a phone at his ear. My dad crouching down on the lawn.

My dad with so much on the line.

My heart does more than pound. My heart beats in the off rhythm you get when you're absolutely out of your mind with fear.

"DeeDee," I hear my father say. "What's up with you? You've got no need of a gun. Let me come inside and we can talk."

But DeeDee Pearson isn't in a mood for conversation.

"No more. No more. People have got to understand I don't deserve this. Teddy deserves better than this," DeeDee says, talking about their kid. "We're all going to be better off if we're not here."

What the hell is it? What's going on? The Pearsons? Just a few weeks ago, Nana dropped off one of her sweet lemon pound cakes for them. The

Pearsons have always been in and out of our house. Funny. Nice.

"Can I come in, Dee? Then we can talk," my dad says.

"Don't make me give you a bullet, too, Alex. Don't you come near me," she says.

As he talks to Mrs. Pearson, my dad inches closer toward the front door. I watch as some of the officers in my line of vision shift their own positions. I think I hear voices in the back of the house. One of the women officers crawls real low at the foundation of the house and positions herself under the smashed window.

I have never seen anything like this in my life. It's as simple as that. It is that step beyond frightened, beyond sick, beyond belief.

It takes a whole minute, but my father makes it to the front door.

He steps inside.

Another minute goes by. Then another.

And we all hear a gunshot.

My insides freeze.

Then a senior officer yells, "Stay where you are! Wait for a signal!"

Wait? What are we waiting for?

I tell myself that the gunshot could not have hit my father. He wasn't close enough. Unless the woman was in the front hall. But maybe she shot her husband. Or maybe I'm wrong about thinking my dad is safe. I want to run inside and see what happened. But I'm as frozen in place as the officers who are obeying their orders.

An old cliché can still be the truth. And the truth is that now the seconds seem like hours. In those seconds I think I hear a helicopter in the distance. I see the rear doors of the ambulances being opened.

I hear a shout. My dad's voice. Loud. Calm. From inside the house.

I try to stifle it, try to stay cool and tough, but a sob of relief escapes from my throat.

"Hold fire," he says.

I need to see him.

And I do. He steps out from the house, out the red front door. His arm is around DeeDee Pearson.

The woman walks slowly with my father. She is leaning her head against his chest. She is sobbing.

My father and Mrs. Pearson walk toward the crowd of officers on the street. I watch as my dad says something to Mrs. P. Then he gives her a hug and hands her over to a woman police officer who handcuffs her.

I can't make out everything my dad tells the officers, but I hear enough to start piecing together what happened: "...lifelong struggle with mental illness...husband said she'd stopped taking her medication...having some paranoid thoughts...I kept her calm, convinced her I was there to help her...got her to put down her gun without even taking out mine..."

I am not frozen in fear, but I just don't want to move. Also, I'm not even sure where I should go, what I should do.

Then I see my father break away from the group of officers he's been talking to. I watch him turn toward the Pearson house. At first I think he's studying the broken window, the red door, the cluster of police standing in front of the house. And then he looks to the side of the house where I'm still crouched near the ground.

As he begins walking toward me, he shouts, "Ali. Come on, son. It's time to go home."

Oh, my God. He knew I was there the whole time.

CHAPTER 43

BETWEEN MY DEBATE anxiety and then the nightmare over at the Pearsons' house, I am totally exhausted. I'm sure of this because when I wake up that weekend on Saturday, it's almost noon. That's incredible for me. Eight a.m. is my usual weekend wake-up time.

What's even more incredible is that the members of my family actually let me sleep till noon. Maybe Dad told them I needed my rest. Or maybe they all had better things to do than get me out of bed.

I pull on my jeans. I check my phone. I open up Instagram and give it a quick scroll. I don't believe it. I see...

Nothing out of the ordinary. Absolutely nothing. No more trash-talking posts about the debate. No more nasty DMs filled with insults and threats. But I do see a new message from Gabe. I open it.

I figured out who made that finsta! Gabe's talking about that @AliCross4Cops Instagram account, the one with all those pictures of police and heart emojis, and that awful photoshopped picture of my dad. Came from same IP address as A-Train's account. So I sent him an anonymous text message to shut it down... or somebody would start posting even worse photoshopped pics of HIM!

That Gabe. What a pal. What a genius. (And A-Train, what a jerk!) I'm happy the mystery is solved. I search for that fake account. Yup, it's gone. I'm about to go back to scrolling when I realize, oh, man, I've got to be at a one o'clock basketball game in the church parking lot. I slip my phone into my jeans pocket and head downstairs.

The house seems to be completely empty. But

Nana hasn't forgotten about me. On the kitchen is a five-piece-high stack of pancakes and a glass of what Nana calls milk-tea, which, as you might have guessed, is a terrific mixture of half tea, half milk, and the perfect amount of sugar, "perfect" being a lot.

Also spread out on the table is a copy of the weekend section of the *Washington Post.* (If you challenge Nana as to why she can't read the *Post* online, she just says, "Ali, I simply prefer my news in a thing called a news*paper.*")

I look at the paper, and I immediately see why it's been left out and opened for me to see. There on the bottom front page is a big article with a great big headline:

DC POLICE: WHOSE SIDE ARE YOU ON?

Pancakes can wait. I've got to read this.

Wow. It turns out to be a kind of more sophisticated version of the same debate Sienna and I just had. Like our debate, it takes up the question of police behavior, but then—I am really pleased to see—it pretty much gives both sides of the argument.

I start reading. One paragraph begins, "Almost every DC citizen we spoke to was frustrated by police methods but also by the rising crime. Yet all agreed that the solution could only come from people on both sides of the issue changing their understanding and..."

Wait a minute!

Now my eye suddenly catches a different headline on a different article. It's an article right next to the one I've been reading. It's not long. Not a huge headline. The headline itself practically knocks me over.

THE DETECTIVE'S SON

MEET ALI CROSS

It's written by someone named Gloria Torres. And after a four-second struggle with my brain, I remember that Gloria Torres is the *Post* reporter who came to our front door a few weeks ago. She's the one who asked me about the First Amendment. And I told her what I thought, but...that I didn't want to be interviewed. She said she'd be back.

But I never saw her again. She managed to write something about me anyway. I begin to read the article...

> Meet the brash young man who's caught between both sides of the "citizens versus the police" debate.
>
> Meet Ali Cross. He is the son of prominent DC detective Alex Cross. But young Cross is also a student in a middle school where valid complaints and disagreement about police brutality echo in the classrooms.
>
> I am told that Ali strives to find the wise middle ground in this vitally important debate. And speaking of debates, just yesterday...

Suddenly my phone chirps. It's an alert from the police scanner app. I guess Gabe reactivated it after all.

I pull out my phone and look down at the screen. There's been a holdup at Garrison's Sporting Goods, a great old store right near our church. It's been there forever. Garrison's is where my dad took me when I was six years old to get my first lace-up sneakers.

I stop. I think.

I'm really dying to finish this newspaper article.

Then there are the pancakes waiting to be eaten.

Don't forget the basketball game.

Everything in my world is piling up.

Plus, after what I witnessed at the Pearson house, I'm not sure I want to put myself in such a dangerous position again. What if Dad had gotten hurt? What if I'd seen it happen?

I almost put my phone away.

Then, all of a sudden, the decision about what to do next becomes very simple and very clear. Just do whatever means the most to you.

Dad does his job. Always. In fact, he's back on the job today.

Maybe it's in my DNA.

I'm out the kitchen door.

I'm on my way to Garrison's.

I'll let you know how it goes.

Daniel X is closing in on his parents' killer. But danger—and the world's deadliest aliens—lurk in the shadows.

TURN THE PAGE TO START READING

AVAILABLE NOW!

True Confessions

IF THIS WERE A MOVIE instead of real life, this would be the part where in a strange, ominous voice I'd say, "Take me to your leader!"

But since *you* are far more important in making a difference in this world than the earth's leaders, and last time I checked on the Internet those leaders seem to have more than enough on their plates, and for the most part I'm not a total dork, I'll just go with a simple "Hi."

My name is Daniel, and this is the first volume of my life story, which, hopefully, will be a very long and distinguished one.

Why should you read it? Very good question.

Maybe because this is your planet, and you have a right to know what's actually happening on it.

And more important, *off* it.

Trust me, there are legions of strange and disturbing creatures out there you probably *don't* want to know about.

Like the fast-breeding creeps with burnt-looking metallic faces and deer horns bristling above hornet noses and stingers, who populate the American Midwest and parts of Europe. Or some very nasty sluglike thingies with jowls like water balloons about to burst all over much of Japan and China, as well as New York City and Vancouver. Plus a host of human-skeletonish freaks with tentacle hair and green multifaceted fly eyes; some white chocolate–colored cretins that look like giant human babies, only with glowing television fuzz for their eyes and mouths; and a praying mantis–looking race with shrunken heads, long red dreadlocks, and a pathetic need to kill, operating in the general area of Texas, Kansas, and Oklahoma.

Maybe I should stop talking, though, before I get too far ahead of myself.

To those of you who feel that you've heard enough, let me say I'm sorry I had to give you a glimpse of what's really out there, and would you please close the cover of this book down tightly on your way out.

Now, the rest of you, I need you to do three important things.

1. Take a deep, deep breath.
2. Disregard everything anyone has ever told you about life on Earth.
3. Turn the page.

One

I WISH THAT I didn't sometimes, but I remember everything about that cursed, unspeakably unhappy night twelve years ago, when I was just three years old and both my parents were murdered.

I was taking an ordinary can of Play-Doh down from the playroom shelf when my mom called from the top of the basement stairs.

"Daniel? Dinner will be ready in five minutes. Time to start wrapping things up, honey."

Finish? Already? I made a face. *But my latest masterpiece isn't done yet!*

"Yes, Mom," I called. "One minute. I'm making Play-Doh history down here."

"Of course you are, dear. I would expect nothing less. Love you. Always."

"Love you back, Mom. Always."

In case you've already noticed that I didn't speak like a typical three-year-old, well, you should have seen what I was building.

I stared at the museum-quality replica of the Lighthouse of Alexandria I was trying to finish.

Behind it, all the way to the edge of my worktable, stood matchless reproductions I'd made of the remaining Seven Wonders of the Ancient World:

The Great Pyramid of Giza
The Hanging Gardens of Babylon
The Statue of Zeus at Olympia
The Temple of Artemis at Ephesus
The Mausoleum of Mausolus
The Colossus of Rhodes

I would have liked to do the Cathedral of Notre Dame and the Chrysler Building as well, but I was only allowed one hour of playtime a day.

I squinted suddenly as I spotted what looked like a tiny, flat black seed climbing up the side of my miniature lighthouse, and really moving too.

Whoa there, little guy! Where do you think you're motoring to?

It was an Arthropoda Arachnida Acari Metastigmata, I thought, recalling the phylum, class, order, and suborder of the tiny creature at a glance. A tick. A young male dog tick, to be exact.

"Hey, little fella," I whispered to the tick. "You on a sightseeing tour?"

Two things happened next, almost simultaneously. Two very odd and unforgettable things.

There was a strange shimmering at the back of my bright, turquoise-blue eyes.

And the tick slowly rose onto its hind legs and said, "Hey, Daniel, my brother, you do real nice work. *Cool lighthouse!*"

About the Author

FOR HIS PRODIGIOUS imagination and championship of literacy in America, **James Patterson** was awarded the 2019 National Humanities Medal, and he has also received the Literarian Award for Outstanding Service to the American Literary Community from the National Book Foundation. He holds the Guinness World Record for the most #1 *New York Times* bestsellers, including *Max Einstein*, *Middle School*, *I Funny*, and *Jacky Ha-Ha*, and his books have sold more than 400 million copies worldwide.

A tireless champion of the power of books and reading, Patterson created a children's book imprint, JIMMY Patterson, whose mission is simple: "We want every kid who finishes a JIMMY book to say, 'PLEASE GIVE ME ANOTHER BOOK.'" He has donated more than three million books to students and soldiers and funds over four hundred Teacher and Writer Education Scholarships at twenty-one colleges and universities. He also supports forty thousand school libraries and has donated millions of dollars to independent bookstores. Patterson invests proceeds from the sales of JIMMY Patterson Books in pro-reading initiatives.